LIBRARY OF DOOM

GRAPHIC NOVELS

THE HOWLING BOOK

TEXT BY
STEVE BREZENOFF

ART BY
JANIO GARCIA
FROM STORM CREATIVE STUDIO

STONE ARCH BOOKS
a capstone imprint

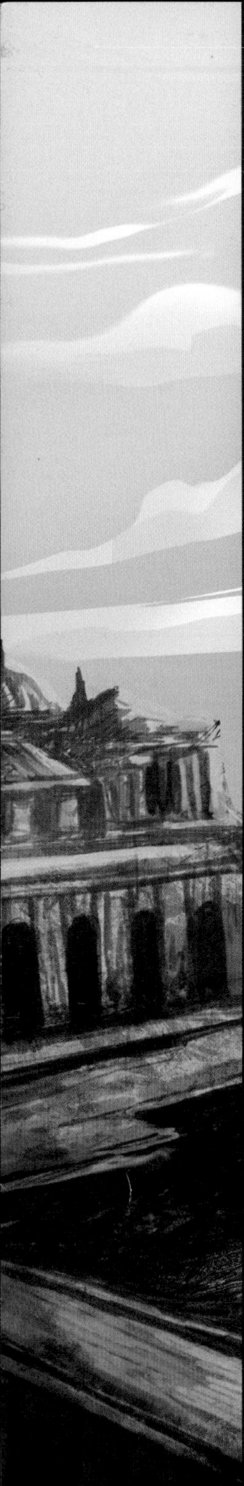

Published by Stone Arch Books, an imprint of Capstone
1710 Roe Crest Drive, North Mankato, Minnesota 56003
capstonepub.com

Library of Congress Cataloging-in-Publication Data
Names: Brezenoff, Steven, author. | Garcia, Janio, illustrator.
Title: The howling book / text by Steve Brezenoff ; art by Janio Garcia.
Description: North Mankato, Minnesota : Stone Arch Books, an imprint of Capstone, 2023. | Series: Library of Doom graphic novels | Audience: Ages 8–11. | Audience: Grades 4–6. | Summary: Shay Isley loves to read but she has become bored by the usual stories so she turns to the horror section and finds the book *Attack of the Moon Beast*; but when night comes, it turns into a monster—part werewolf and part book—and only the Librarian can save her and her little brother from becoming its prey.
Identifiers: LCCN 2022004743 (print) | LCCN 2022004744 (ebook) | ISBN 9781666346220 (hardcover) | ISBN 9781666346244 (paperback) | ISBN 9781666346251 (pdf) | ISBN 9781666346275 (kindle edition)
Subjects: LCSH: Werewolves—Comic books, strips, etc. | Werewolves—Juvenile fiction. | Books and reading—Comic books, strips, etc. | Books and reading—Juvenile fiction. | Librarians—Comic books, strips, etc. | Librarians—Juvenile fiction. | Horror tales. | Graphic novels. | CYAC: Werewolves—Fiction. | Books and reading—Fiction. | Librarians—Fiction. | Horror stories. | Graphic novels. | LCGFT: Graphic novels. | Horror fiction.
Classification: LCC PZ7.7.B748 How 2022 (print) | LCC PZ7.7.B748 (ebook) | DDC 741.5/973—dc23/eng/20220208
LC record available at https://lccn.loc.gov/2022004743
LC ebook record available at https://lccn.loc.gov/2022004744

Designer: Hilary Wacholz
Editor: Abby Huff

This series of graphic novels is dedicated to the memory of Brandon Terrell. I thought of him often while writing these stories. —SB

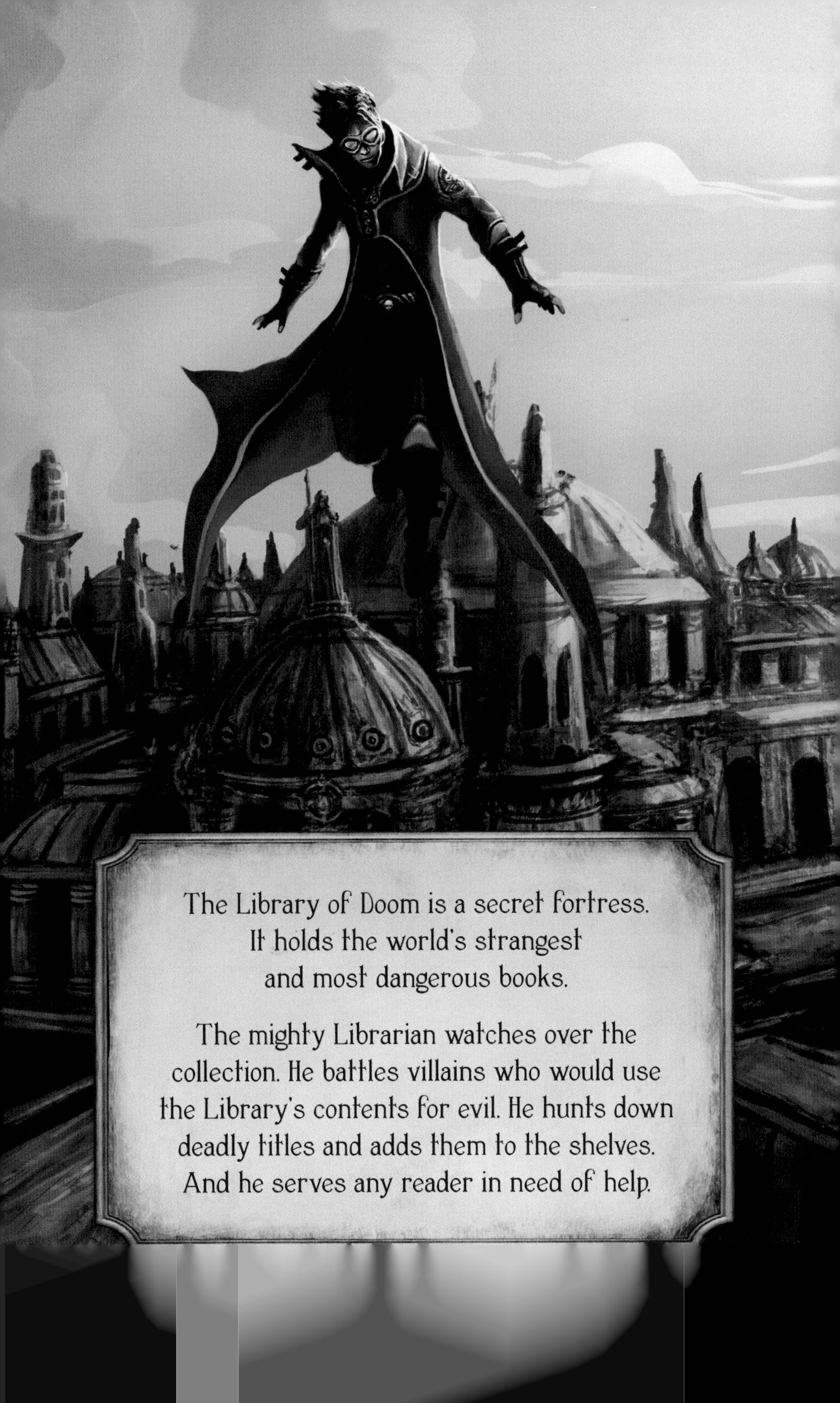

The Library of Doom is a secret fortress.
It holds the world's strangest
and most dangerous books.

The mighty Librarian watches over the collection. He battles villains who would use the Library's contents for evil. He hunts down deadly titles and adds them to the shelves. And he serves any reader in need of help.

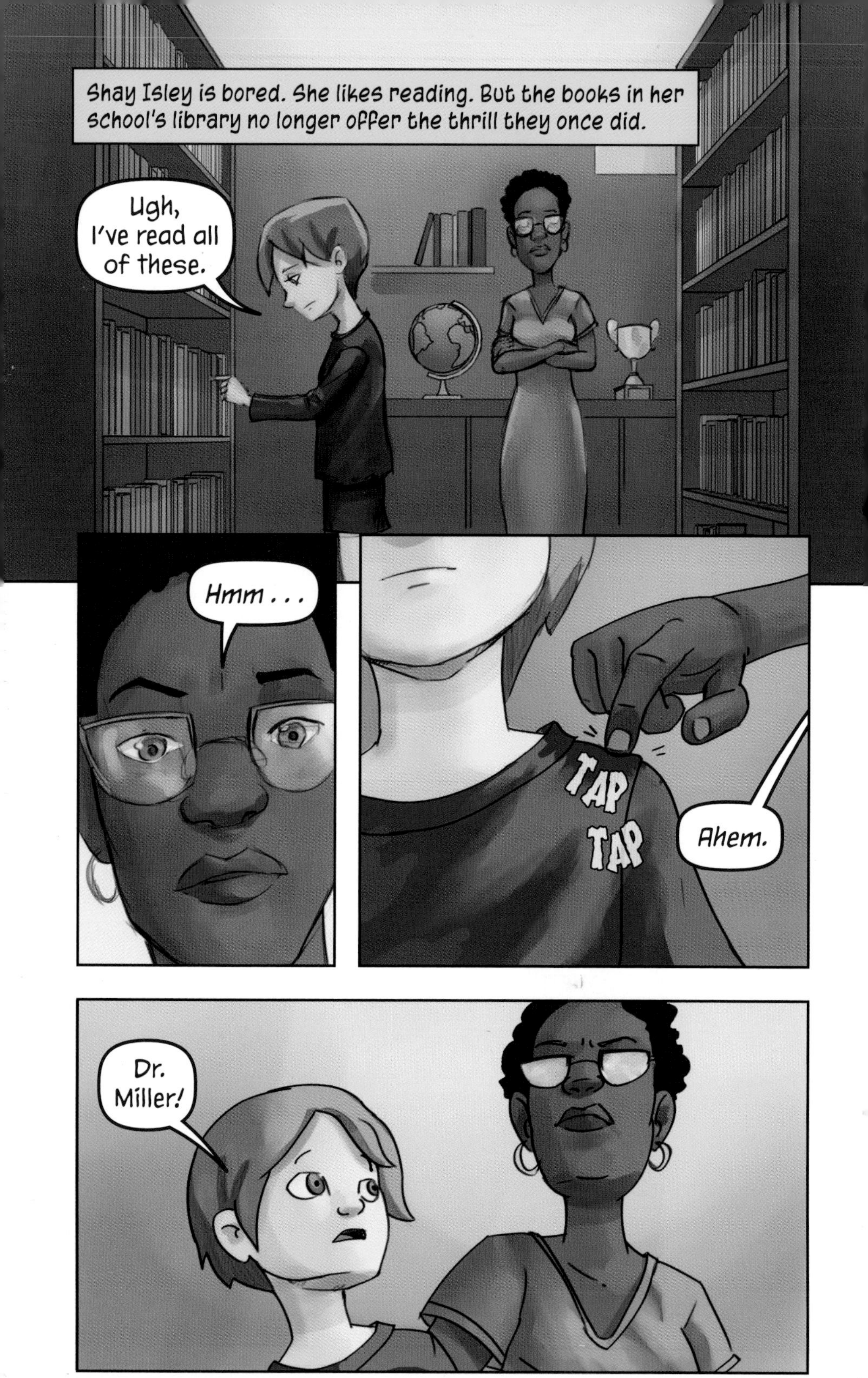
Shay Isley is bored. She likes reading. But the books in her school's library no longer offer the thrill they once did.
Ugh, I've read all of these.
Hmm . . .
TAP TAP
Ahem.
Dr. Miller!

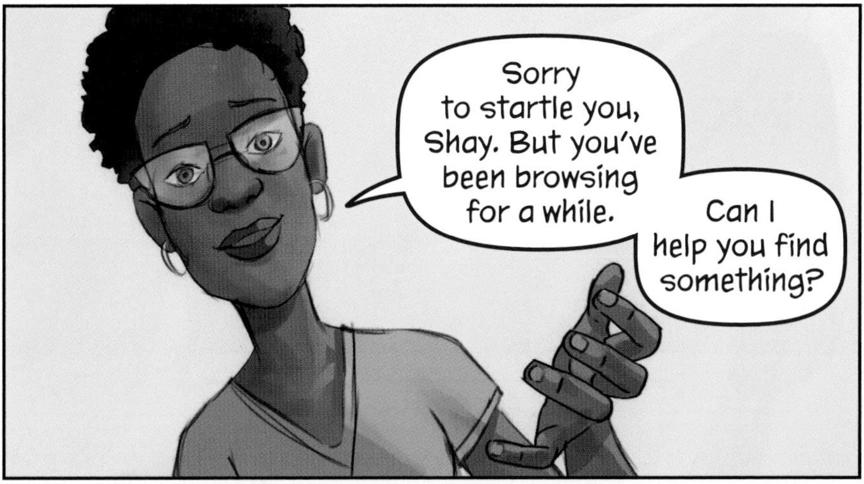
Sorry to startle you, Shay. But you've been browsing for a while.
Can I help you find something?

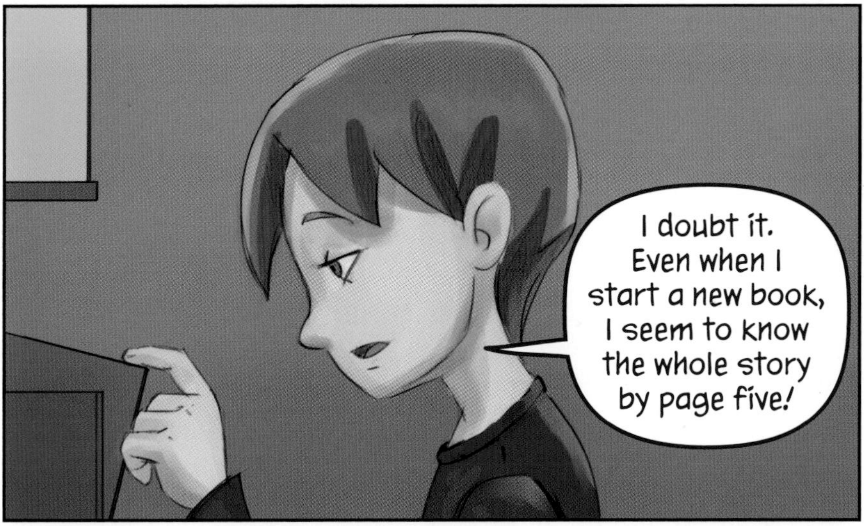
I doubt it. Even when I start a new book, I seem to know the whole story by page five!

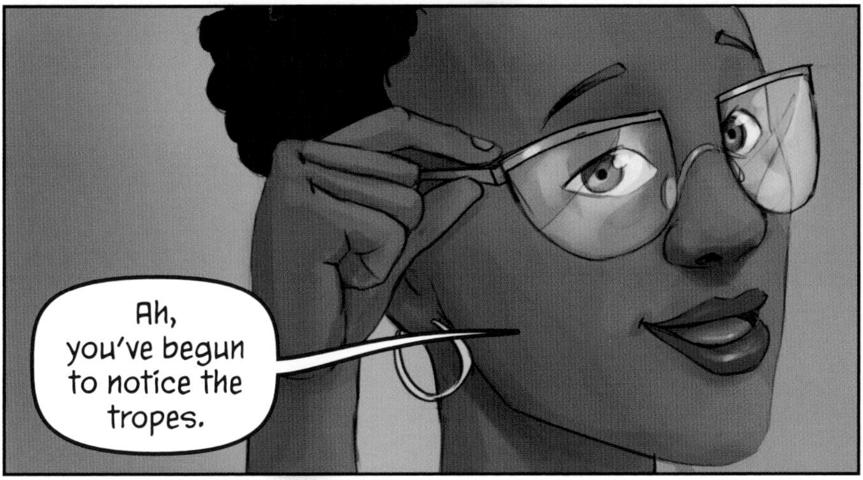
Ah, you've begun to notice the tropes.

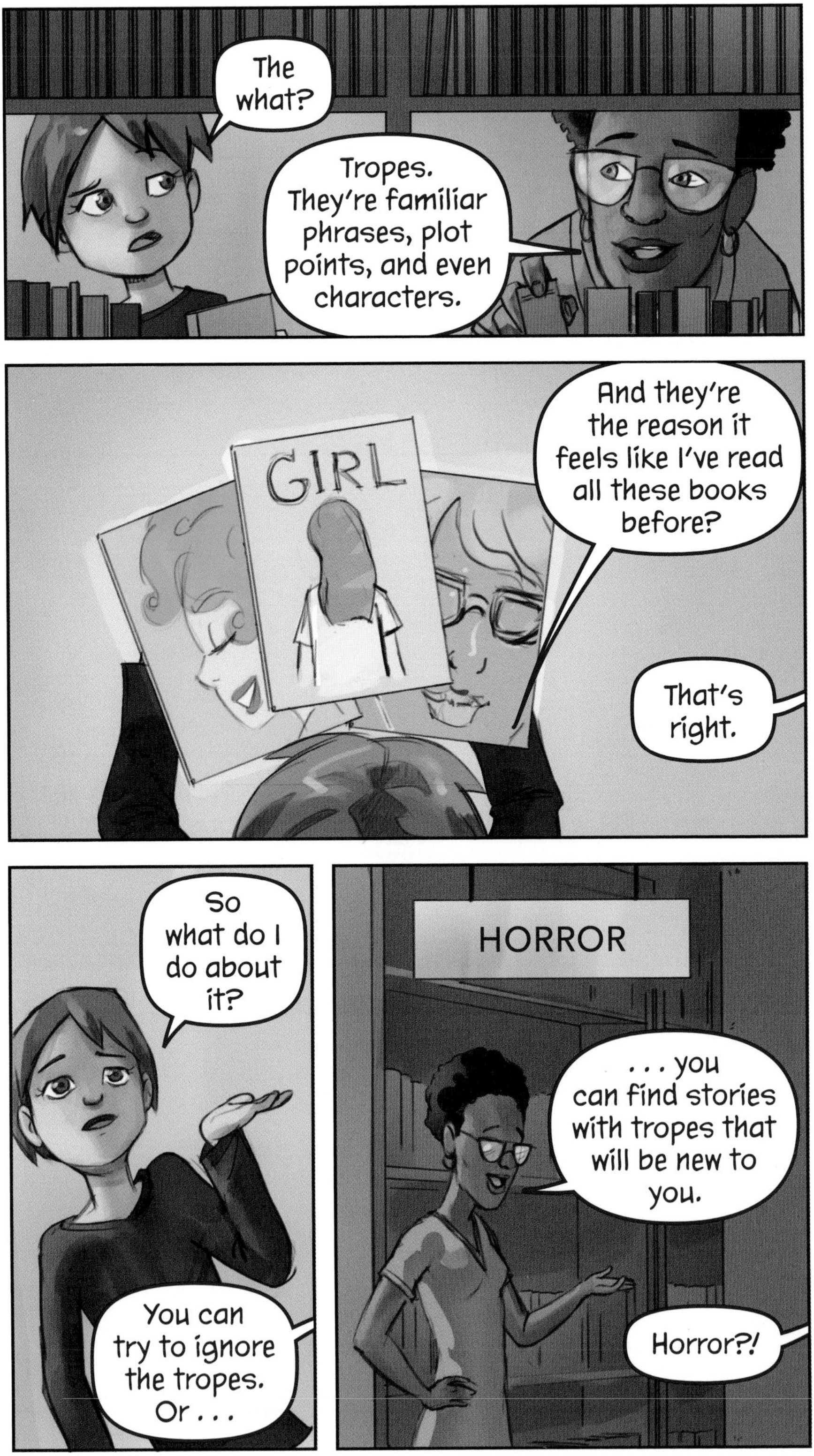
The what?
Tropes. They're familiar phrases, plot points, and even characters.
GIRL
And they're the reason it feels like I've read all these books before?
That's right.
So what do I do about it?
You can try to ignore the tropes. Or . . .
HORROR
. . . you can find stories with tropes that will be new to you.
Horror?!

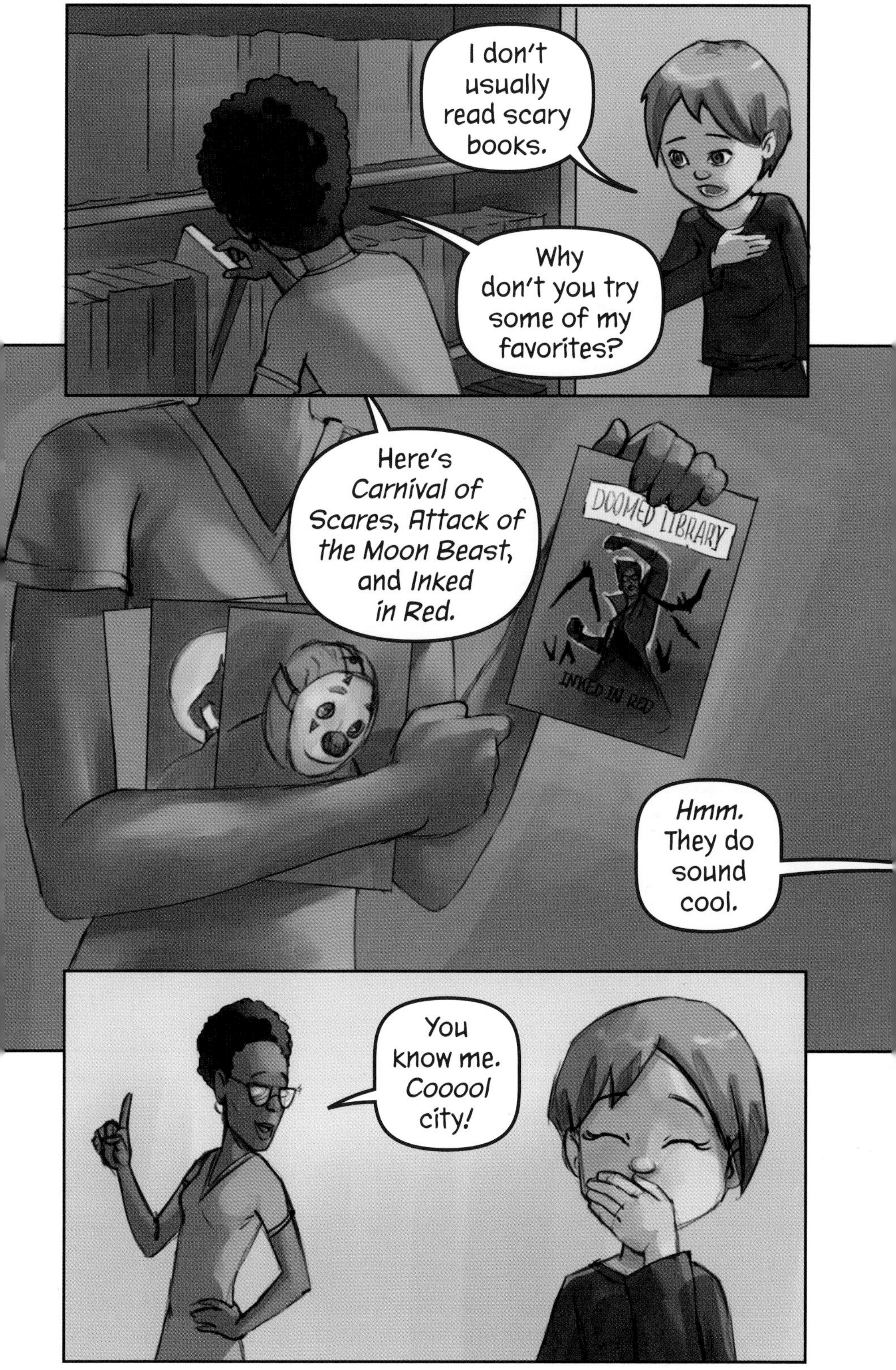
I don't usually read scary books.
Why don't you try some of my favorites?
Here's Carnival of Scares, Attack of the Moon Beast, and Inked in Red.
DOOMED LIBRARY
INKED IN RED
Hmm. They do sound cool.
You know me. Cooool city!

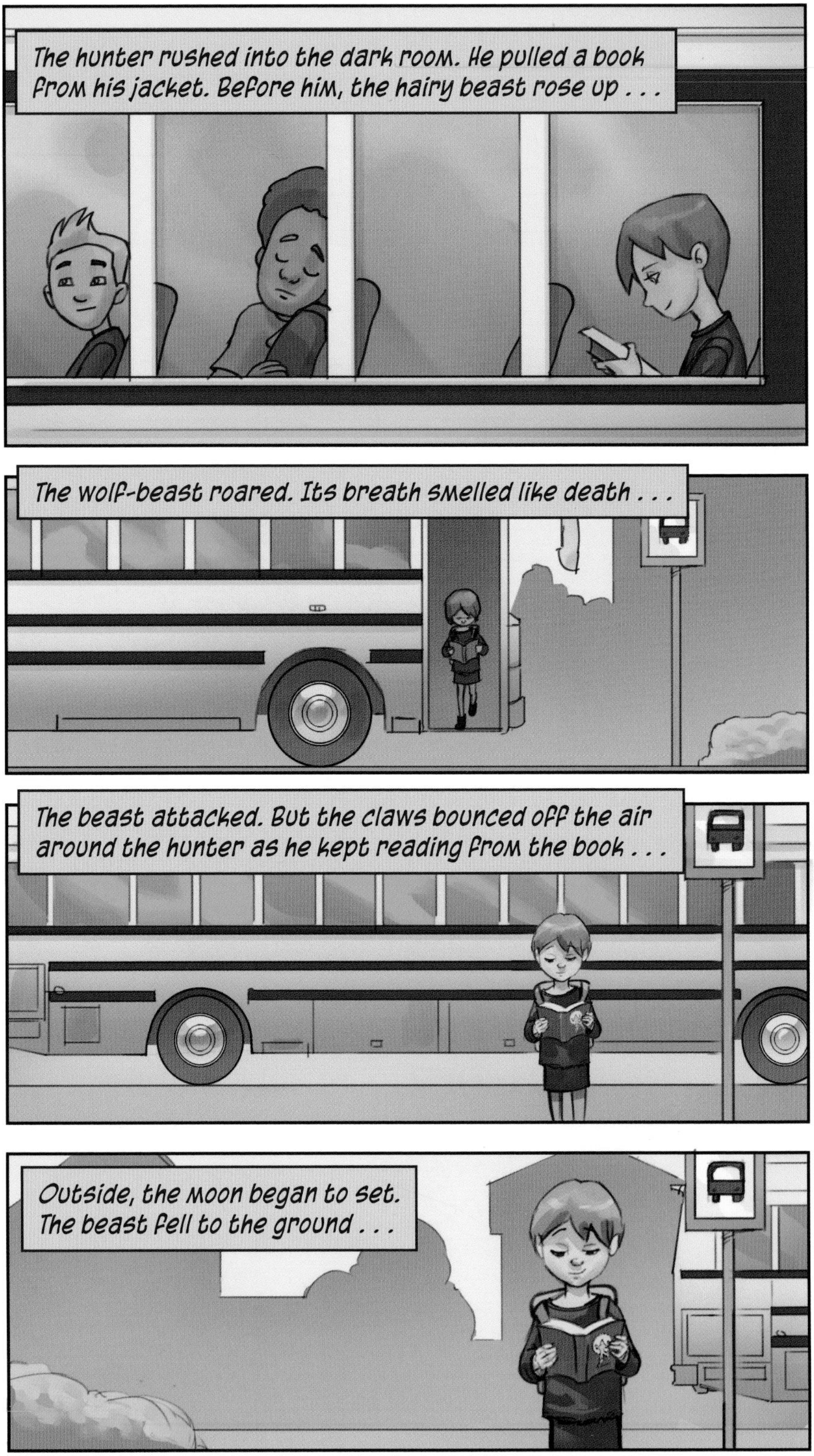
The hunter rushed into the dark room. He pulled a book from his jacket. Before him, the hairy beast rose up . . .
The wolf-beast roared. Its breath smelled like death . . .
The beast attacked. But the claws bounced off the air around the hunter as he kept reading from the book . . .
Outside, the moon began to set. The beast fell to the ground . . .

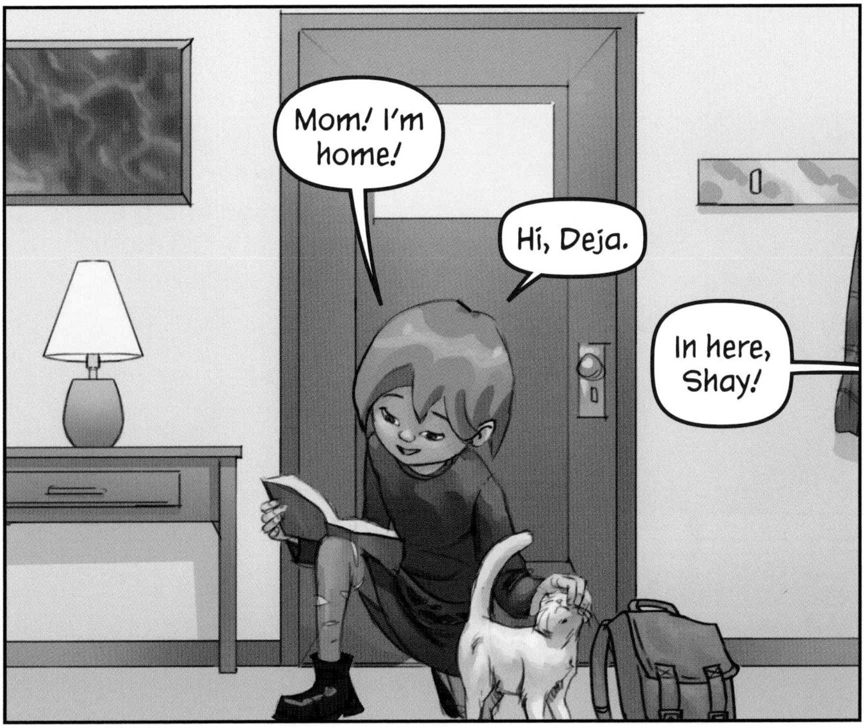
Mom! I'm home!
Hi, Deja.
In here, Shay!

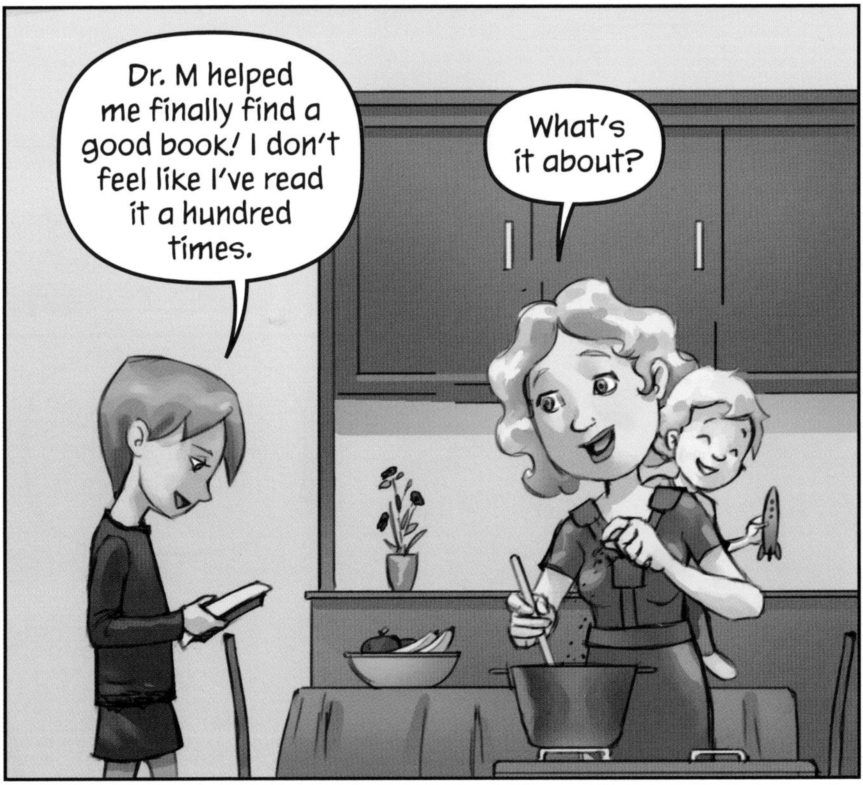
Dr. M helped me finally find a good book! I don't feel like I've read it a hundred times.
What's it about?

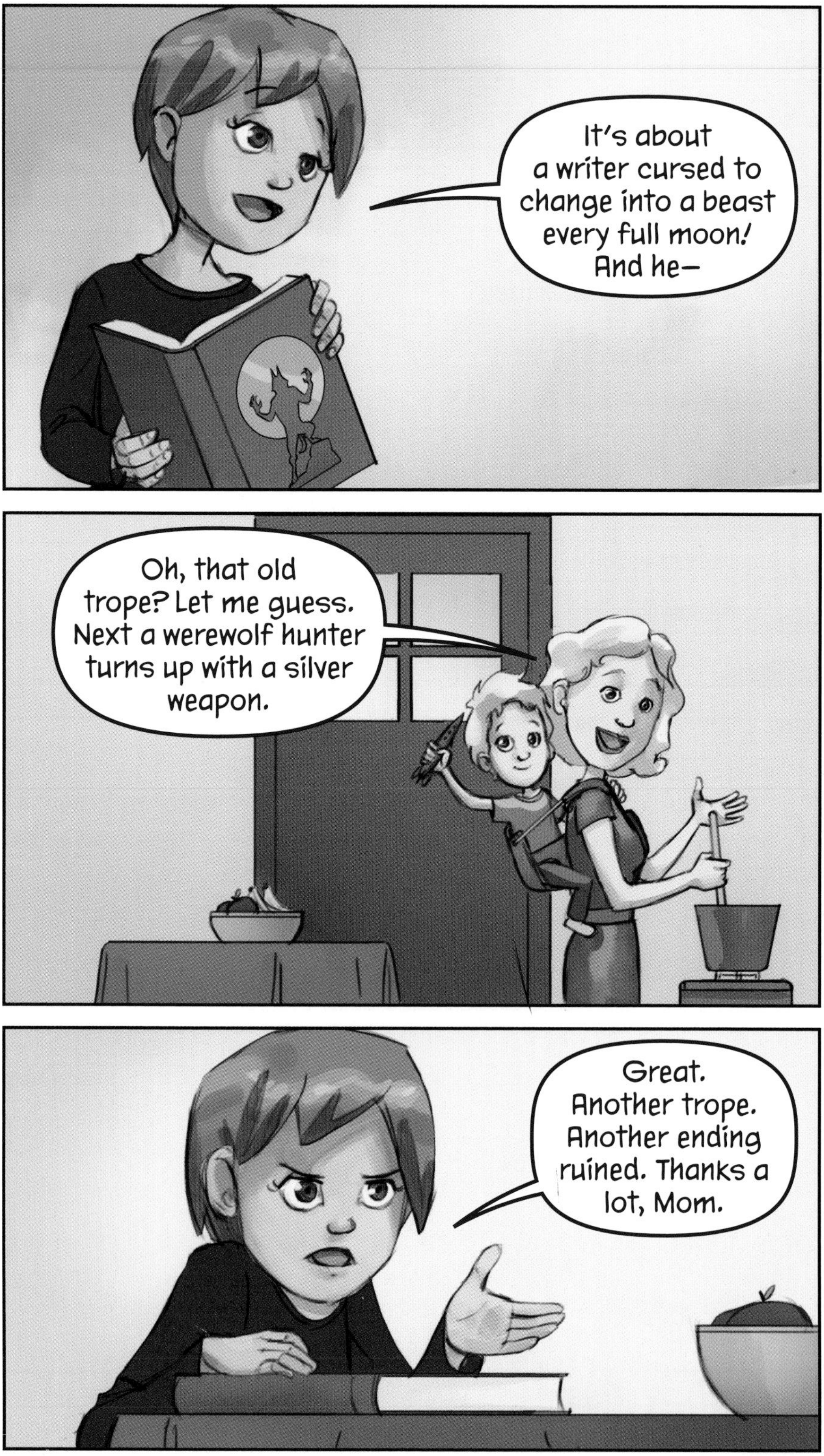
It's about a writer cursed to change into a beast every full moon! And he—
Oh, that old trope? Let me guess. Next a werewolf hunter turns up with a silver weapon.
Great. Another trope. Another ending ruined. Thanks a lot, Mom.

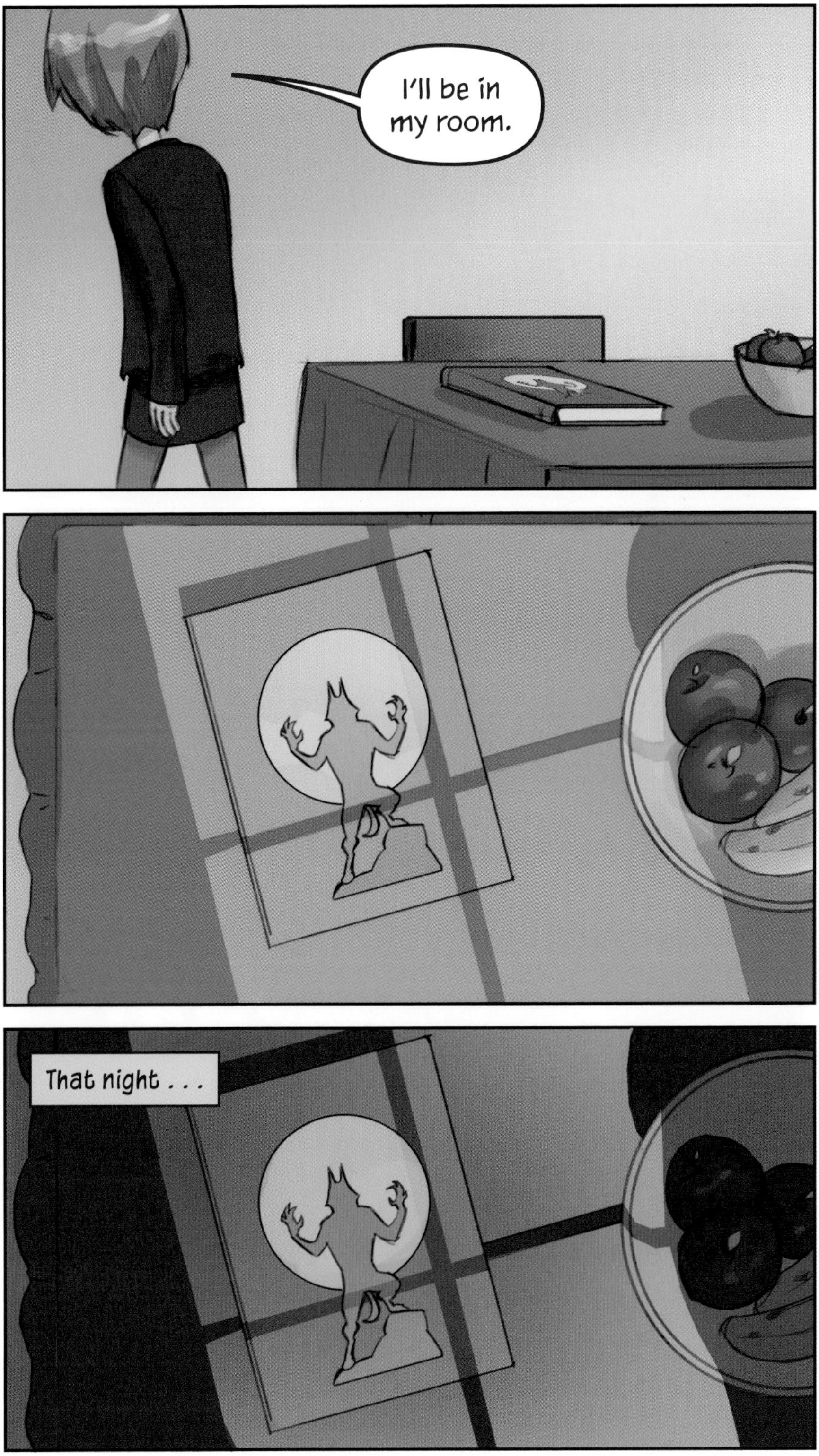
I'll be in my room.
That night . . .

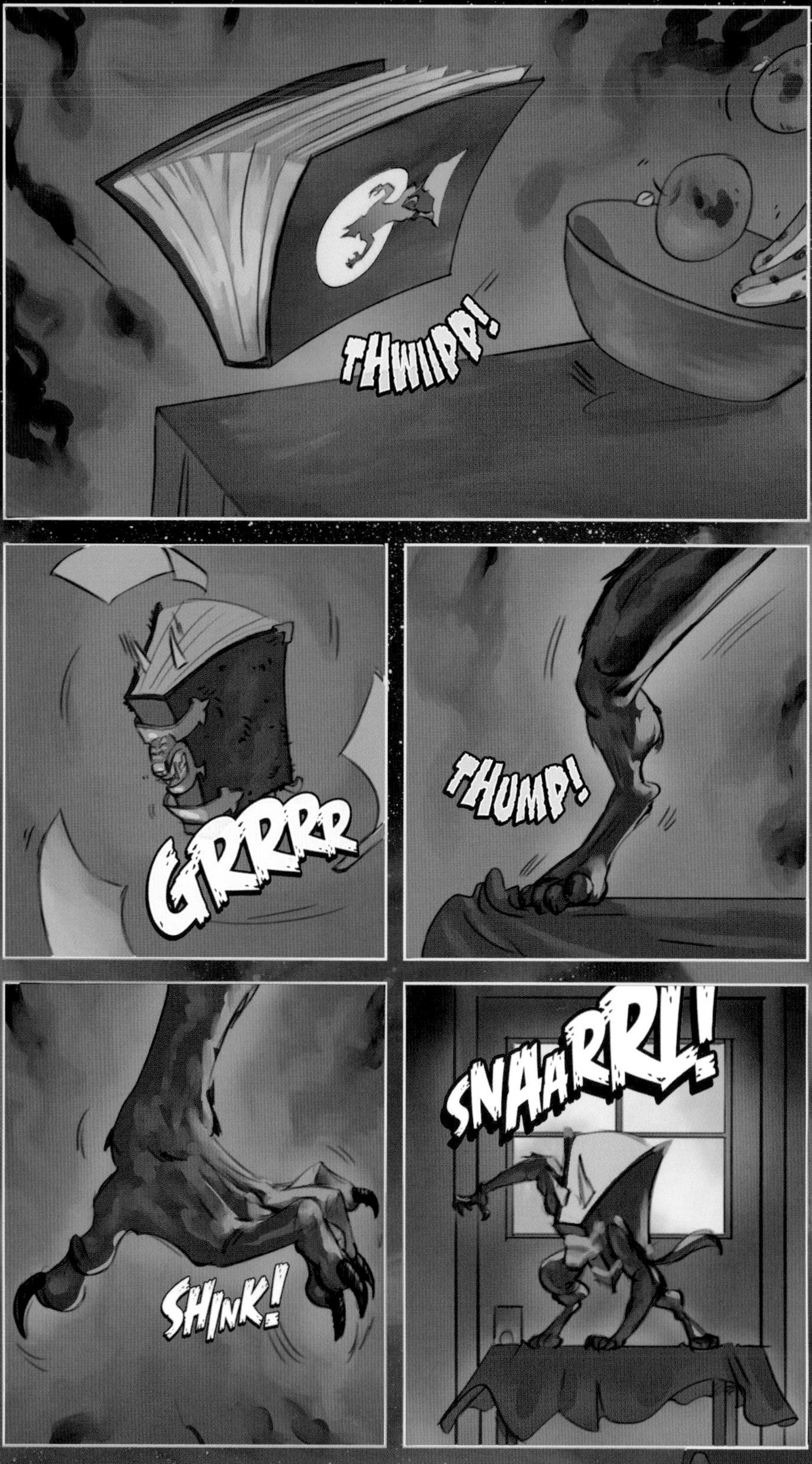
THWIIPP!
GRRRR
THUMP!
SHINK!
SNAARRL!

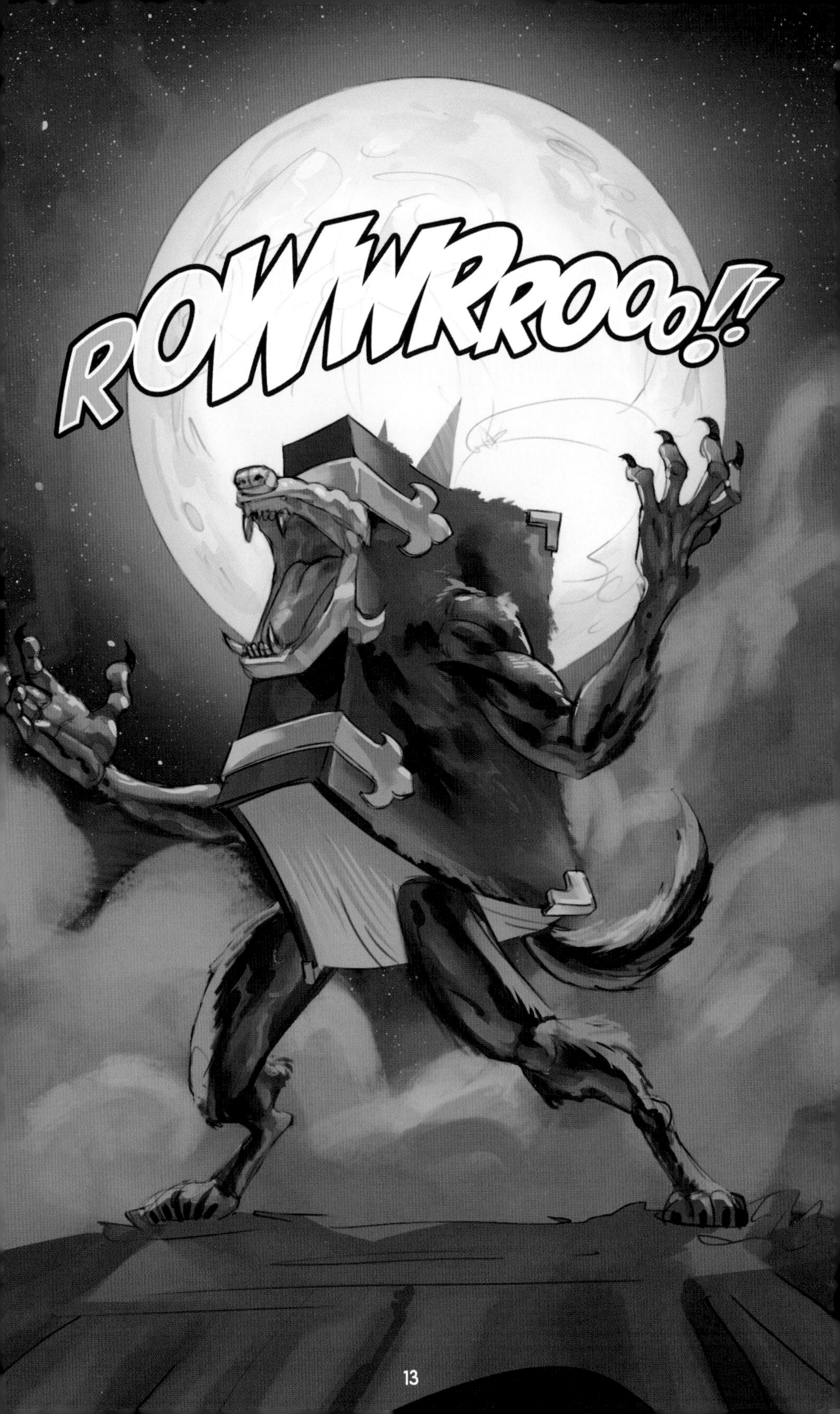
ROWWRROOO!!

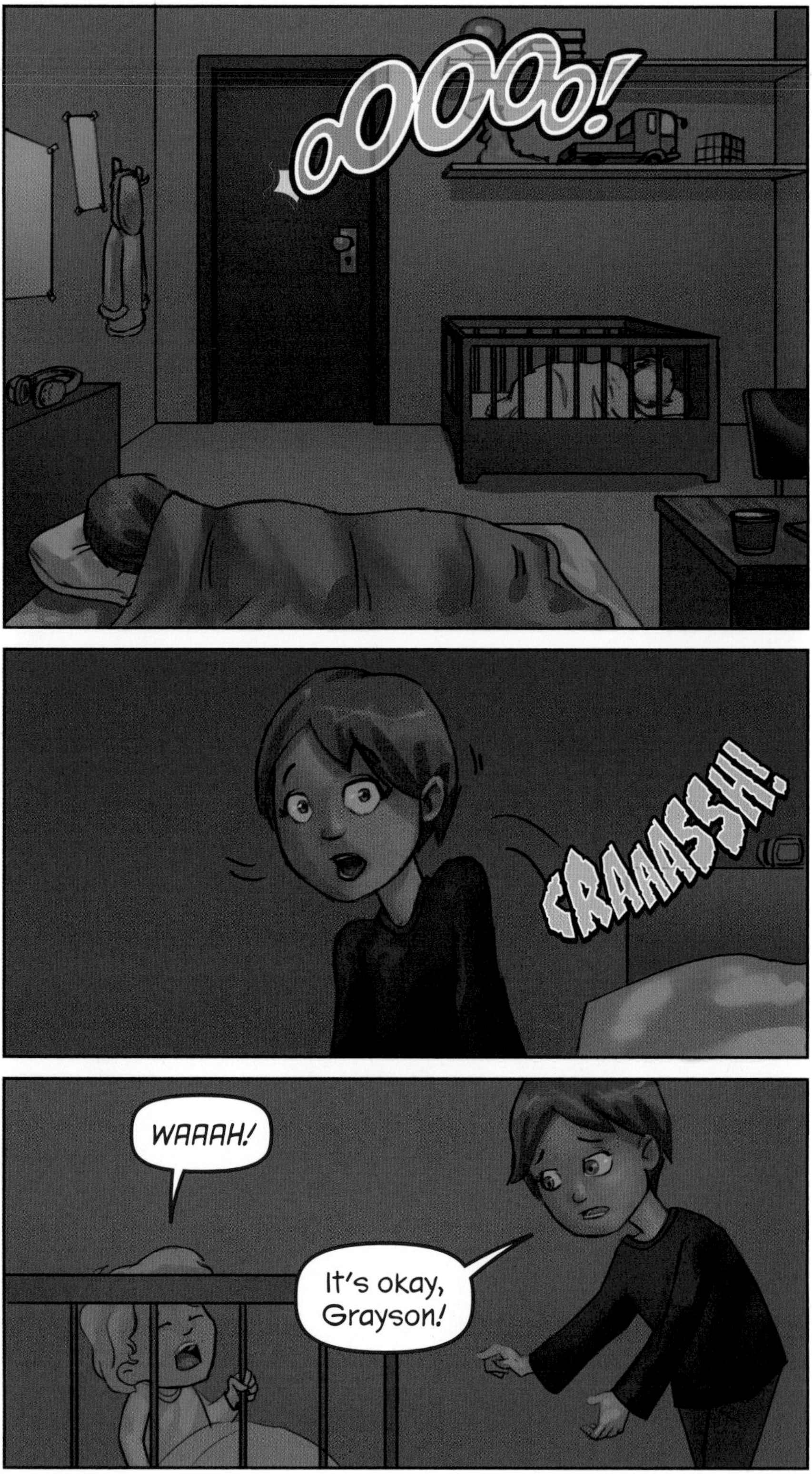
oOOOo!
CRAAASH!
WAAAH!
It's okay, Grayson!

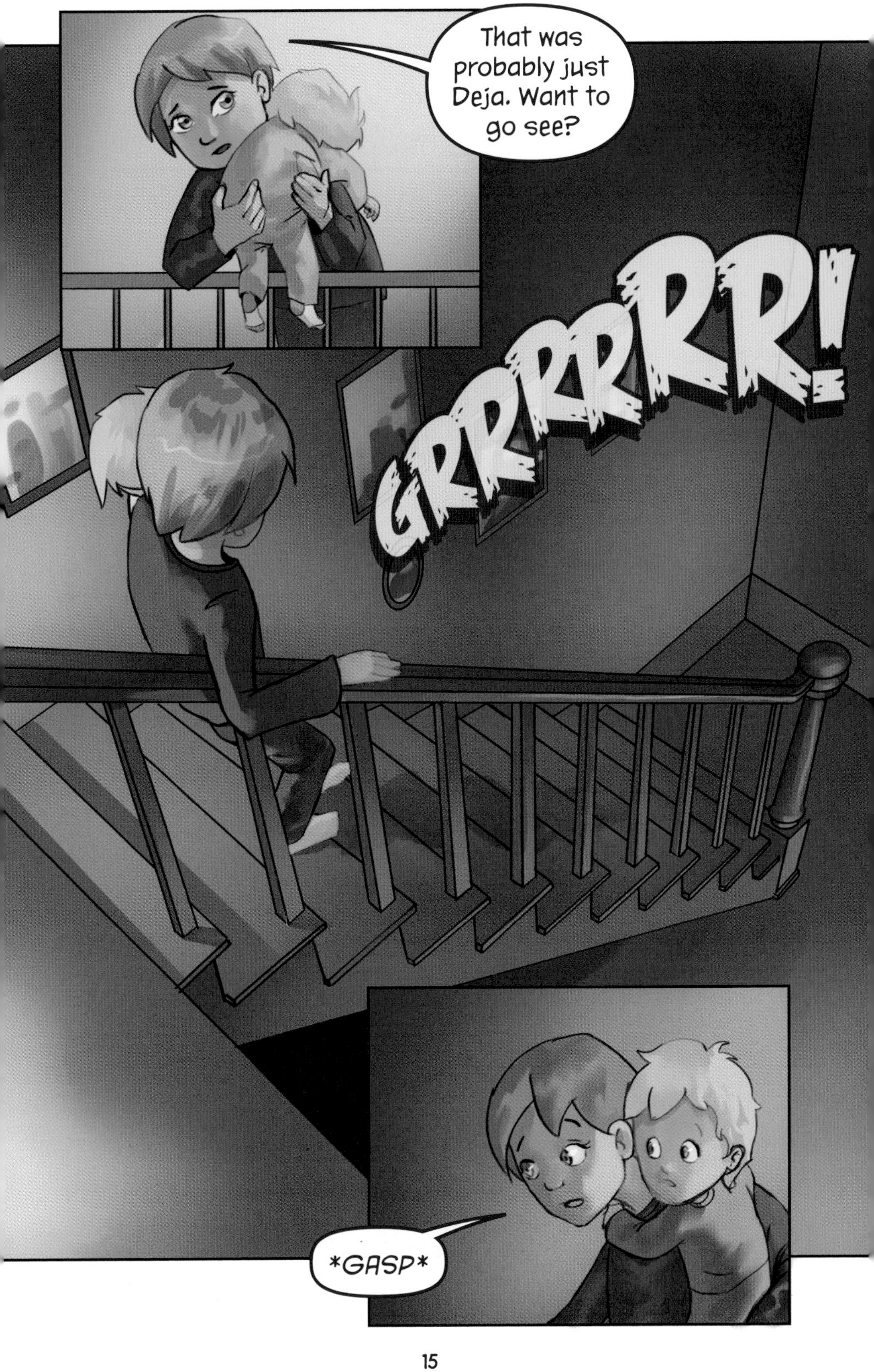
That was probably just Deja. Want to go see?
GRRRRRR!
GASP

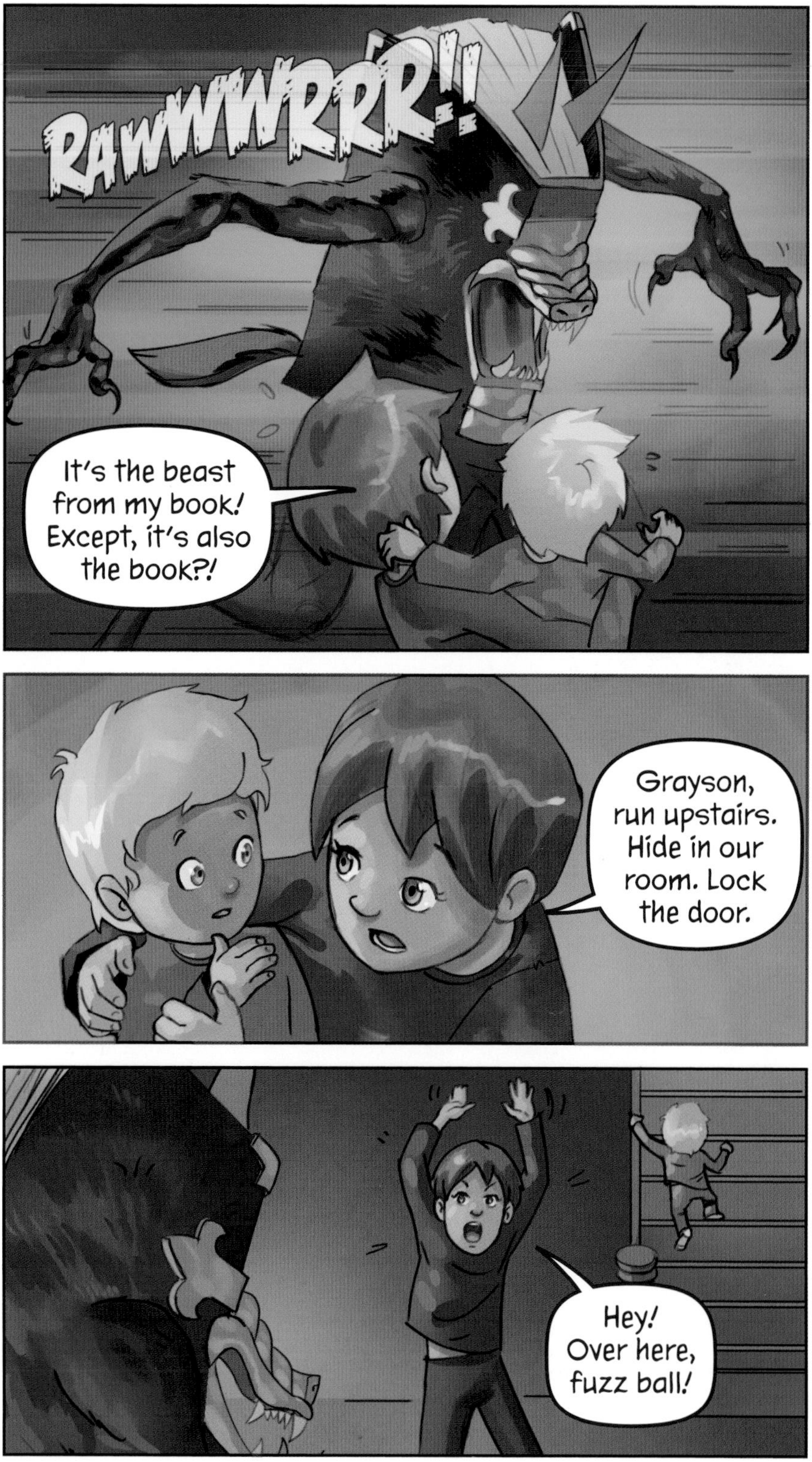
RAWWWRRR!!
It's the beast from my book! Except, it's also the book?!
Grayson, run upstairs. Hide in our room. Lock the door.
Hey! Over here, fuzz ball!

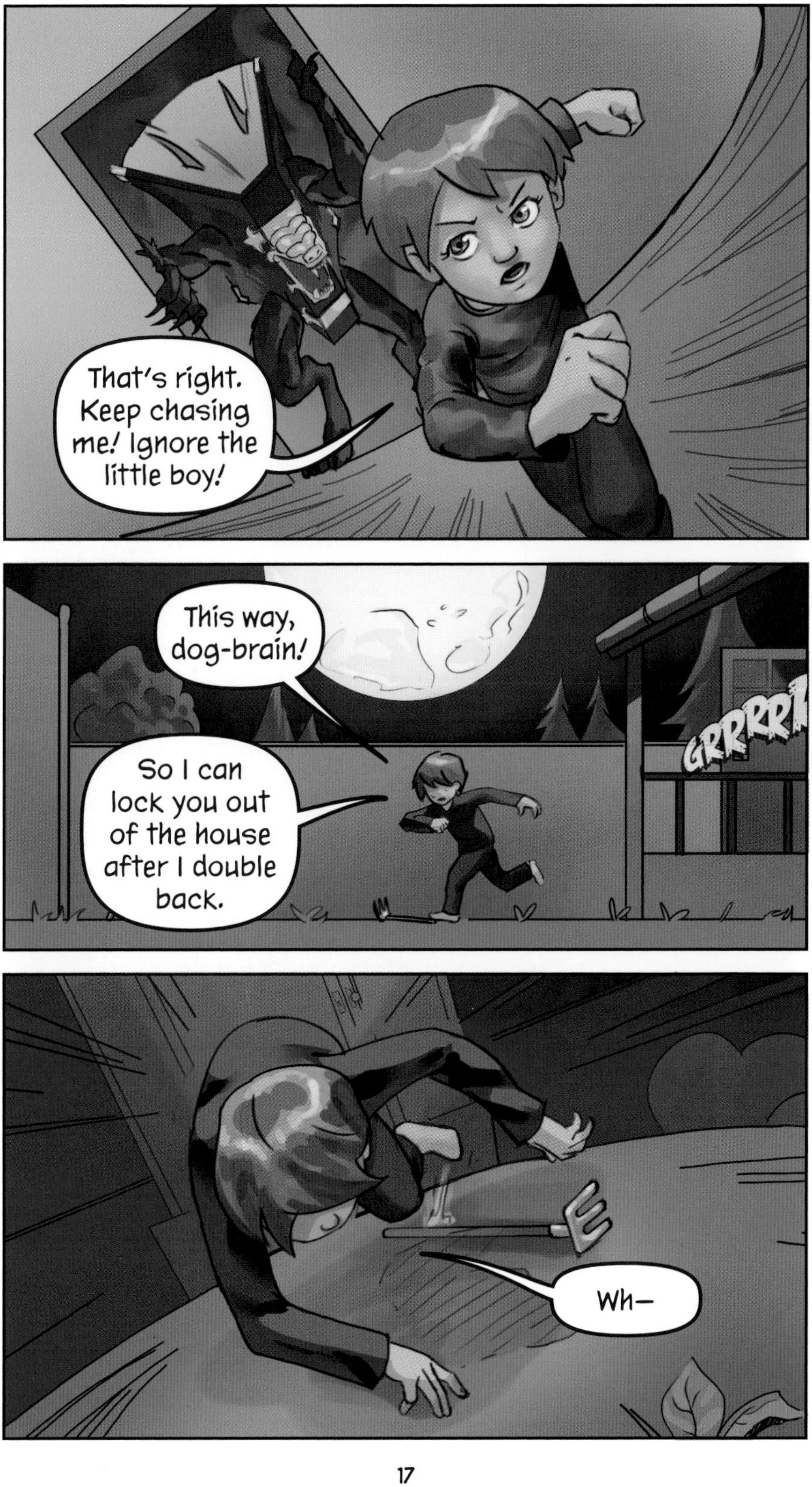
That's right. Keep chasing me! Ignore the little boy!
This way, dog-brain!
So I can lock you out of the house after I double back.
GRRRR
Wh–

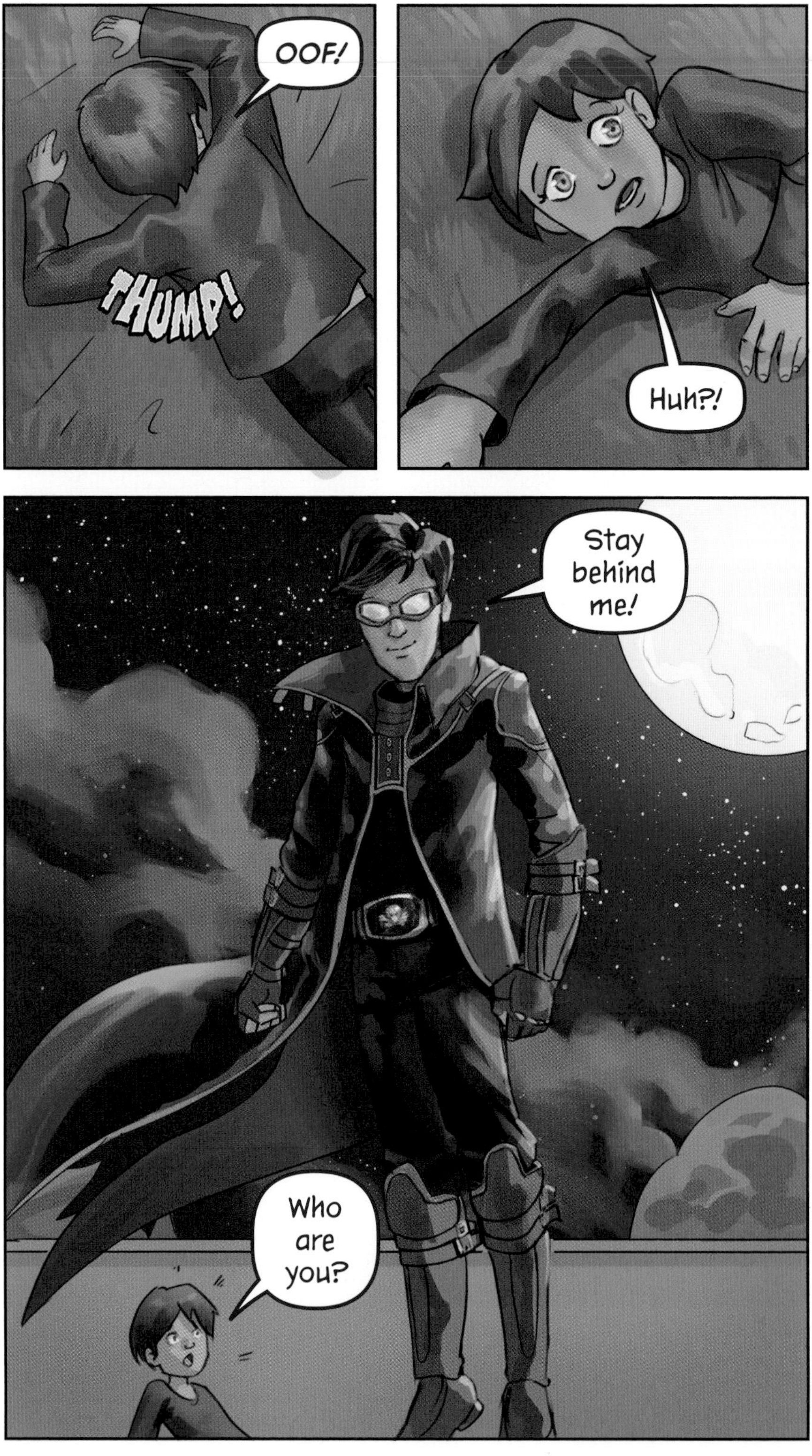
OOF!
THUMP!
Huh?!
Stay behind me!
Who are you?

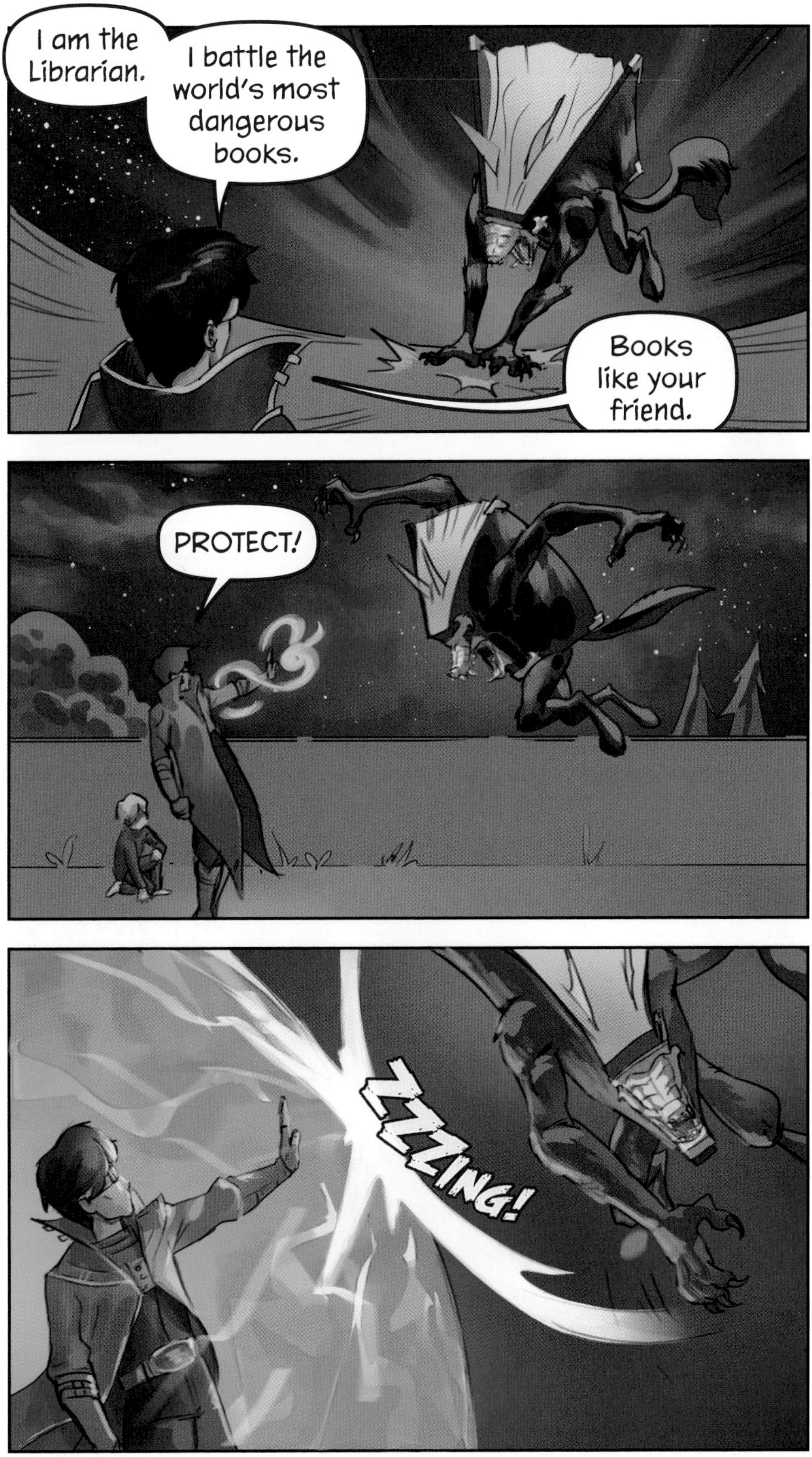
I am the Librarian.
I battle the world's most dangerous books.
Books like your friend.
PROTECT!
ZZZING!

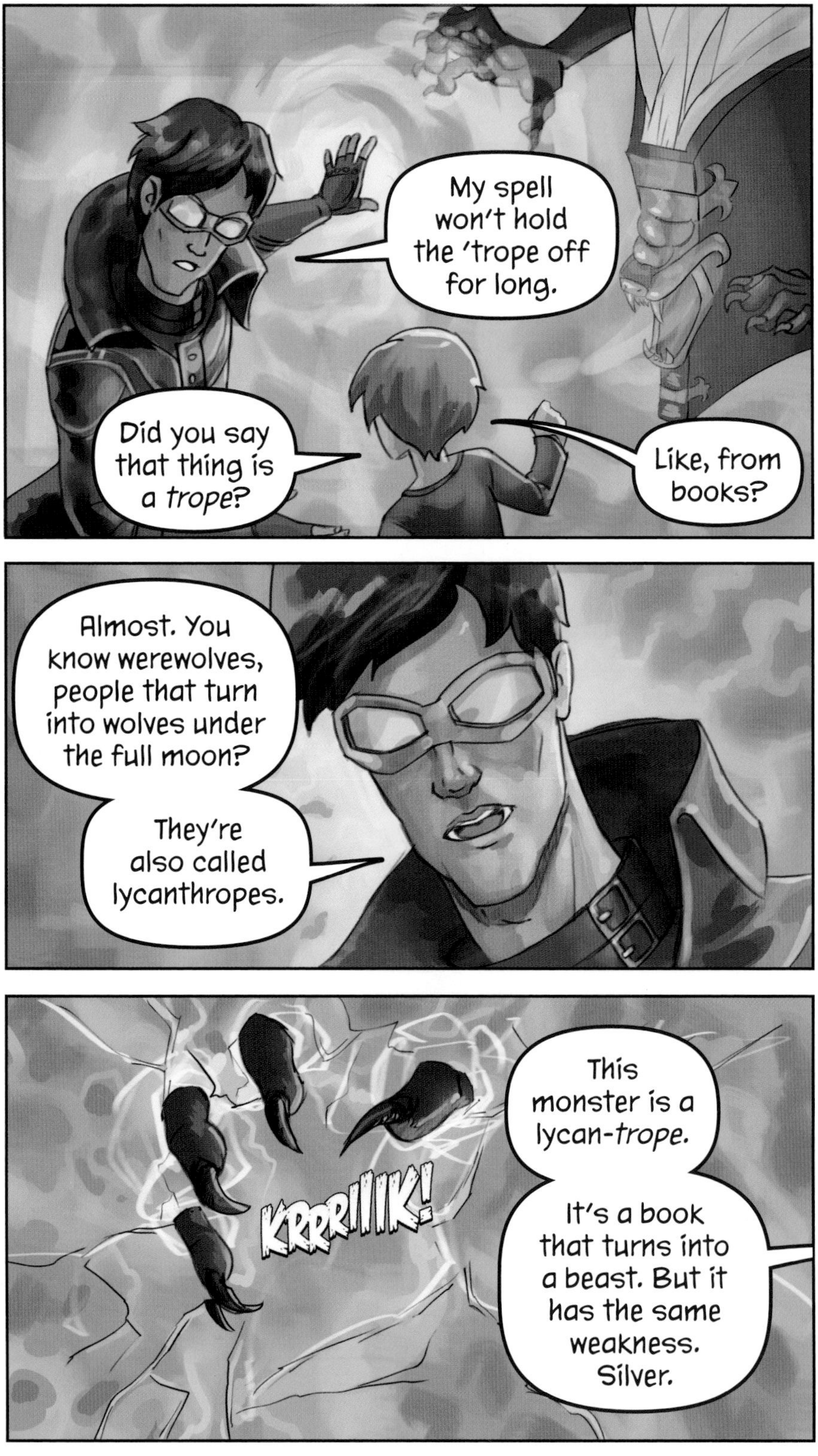

My spell won't hold the 'trope off for long.
Did you say that thing is a *trope*?
Like, from books?
Almost. You know werewolves, people that turn into wolves under the full moon?
They're also called lycanthropes.
This monster is a lycan-*trope*.
KRRRIIIK!
It's a book that turns into a beast. But it has the same weakness. Silver.

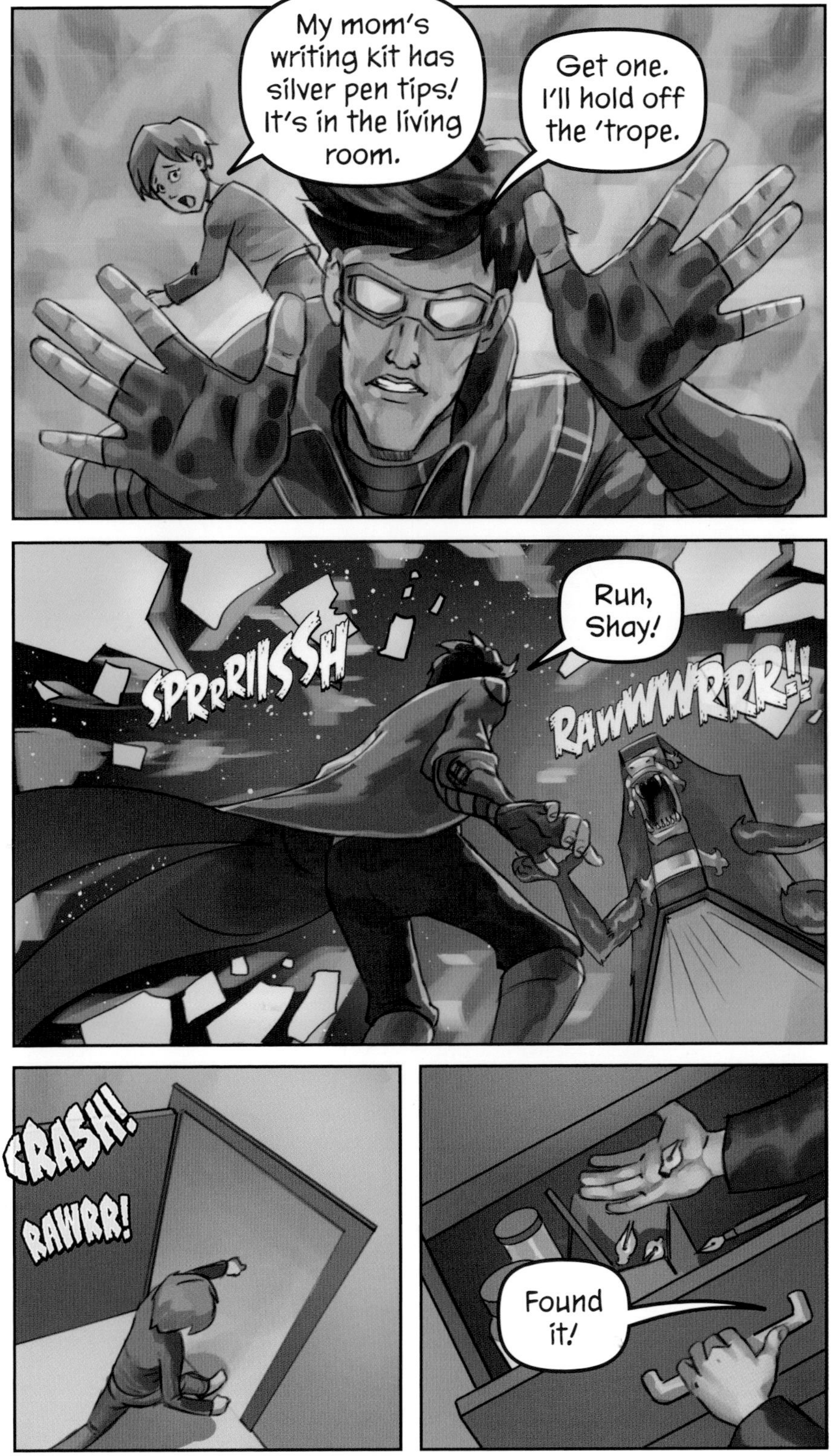
My mom's writing kit has silver pen tips! It's in the living room.
Get one. I'll hold off the 'trope.
SPRRRIISSH
Run, Shay!
RAWWWRRR!!
CRASH!
RAWRR!
Found it!

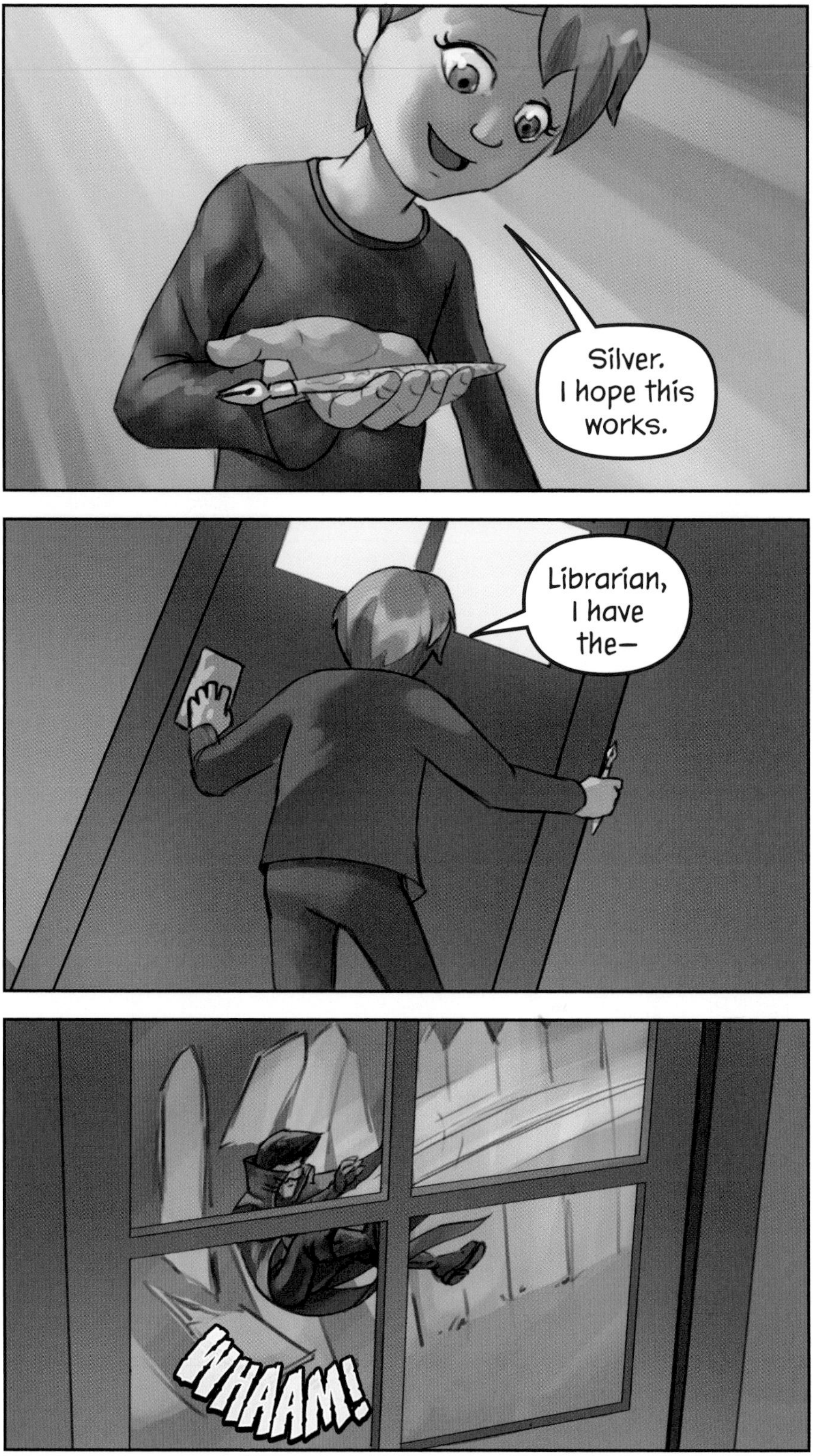
Silver. I hope this works.
Librarian, I have the—
WHAAM!

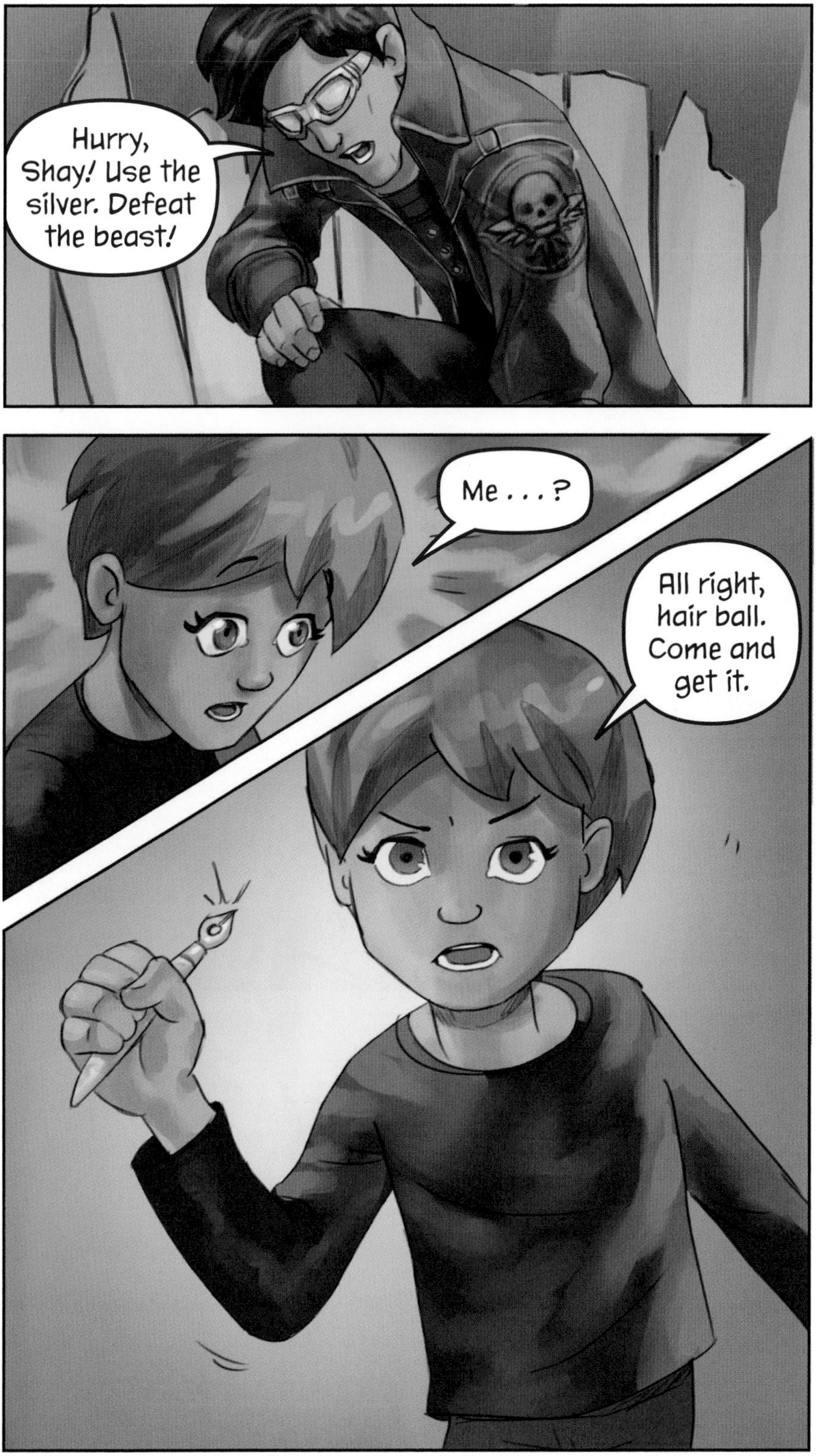
Hurry, Shay! Use the silver. Defeat the beast!
Me . . . ?
All right, hair ball. Come and get it.

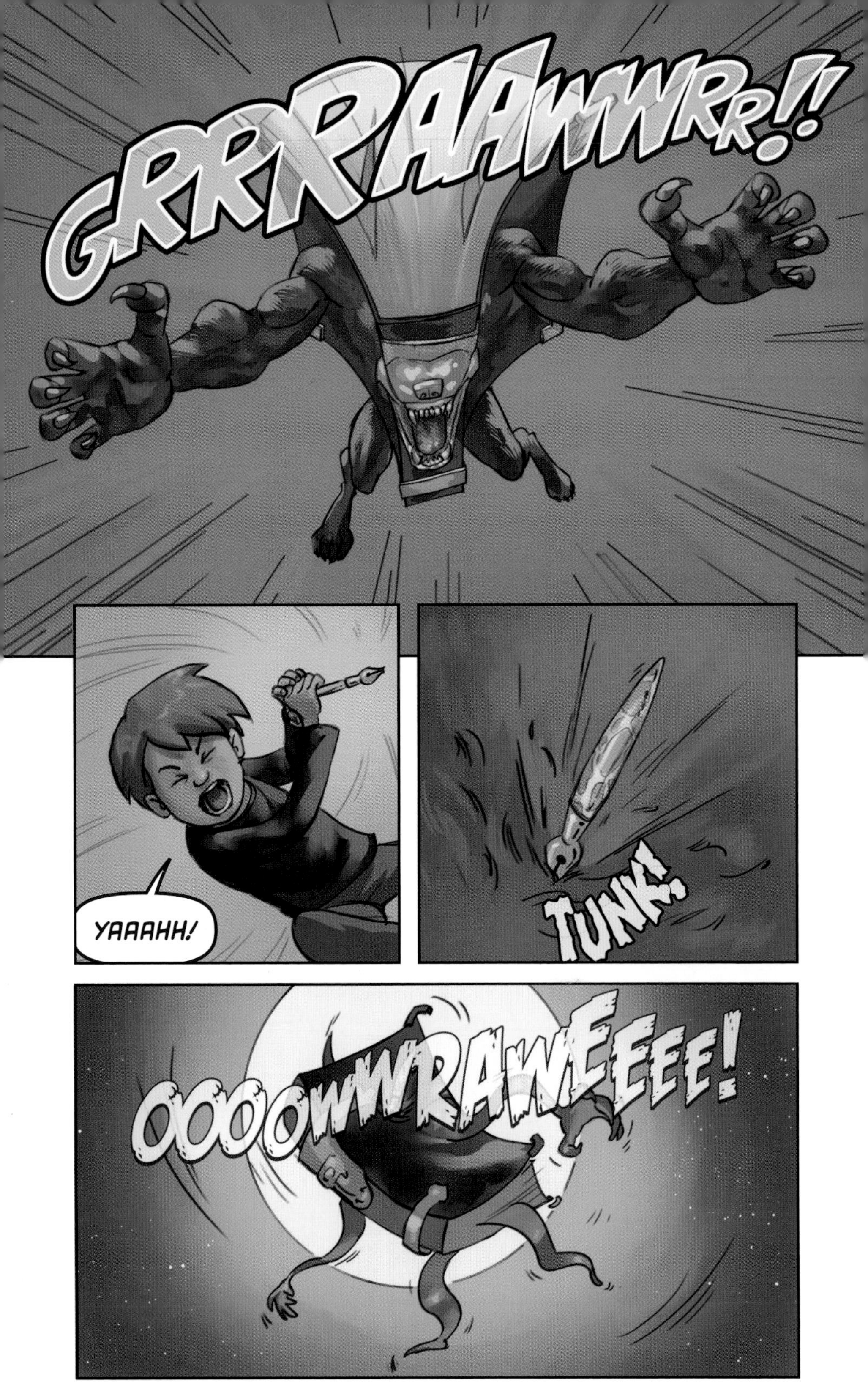
GRRRAAWWRR!!
YAAAHH!
TUNK!
OOOOWWRAWEEEE!

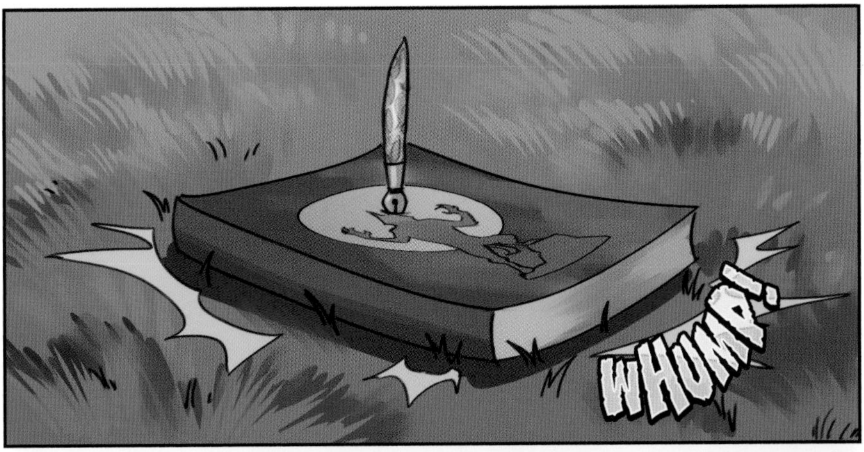
WHUMP!

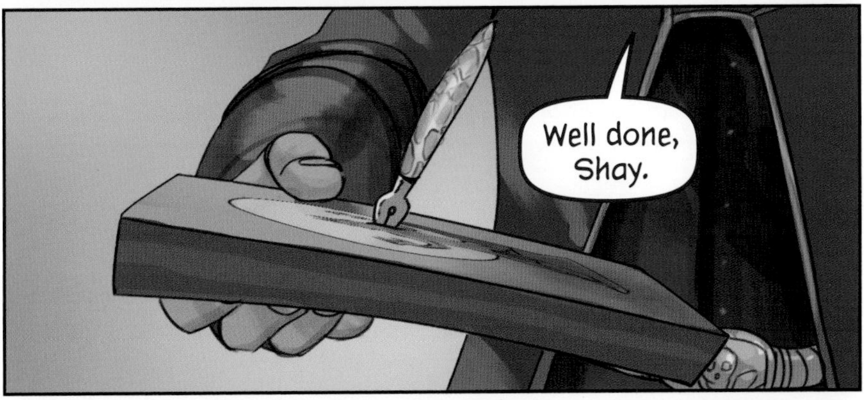
Well done, Shay.

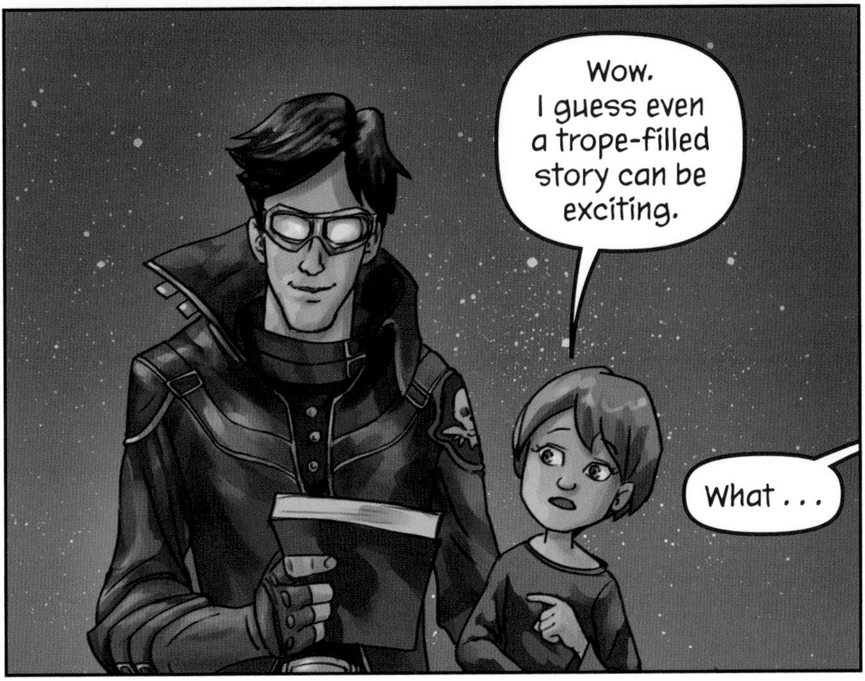
Wow. I guess even a trope-filled story can be exciting.
What . . .

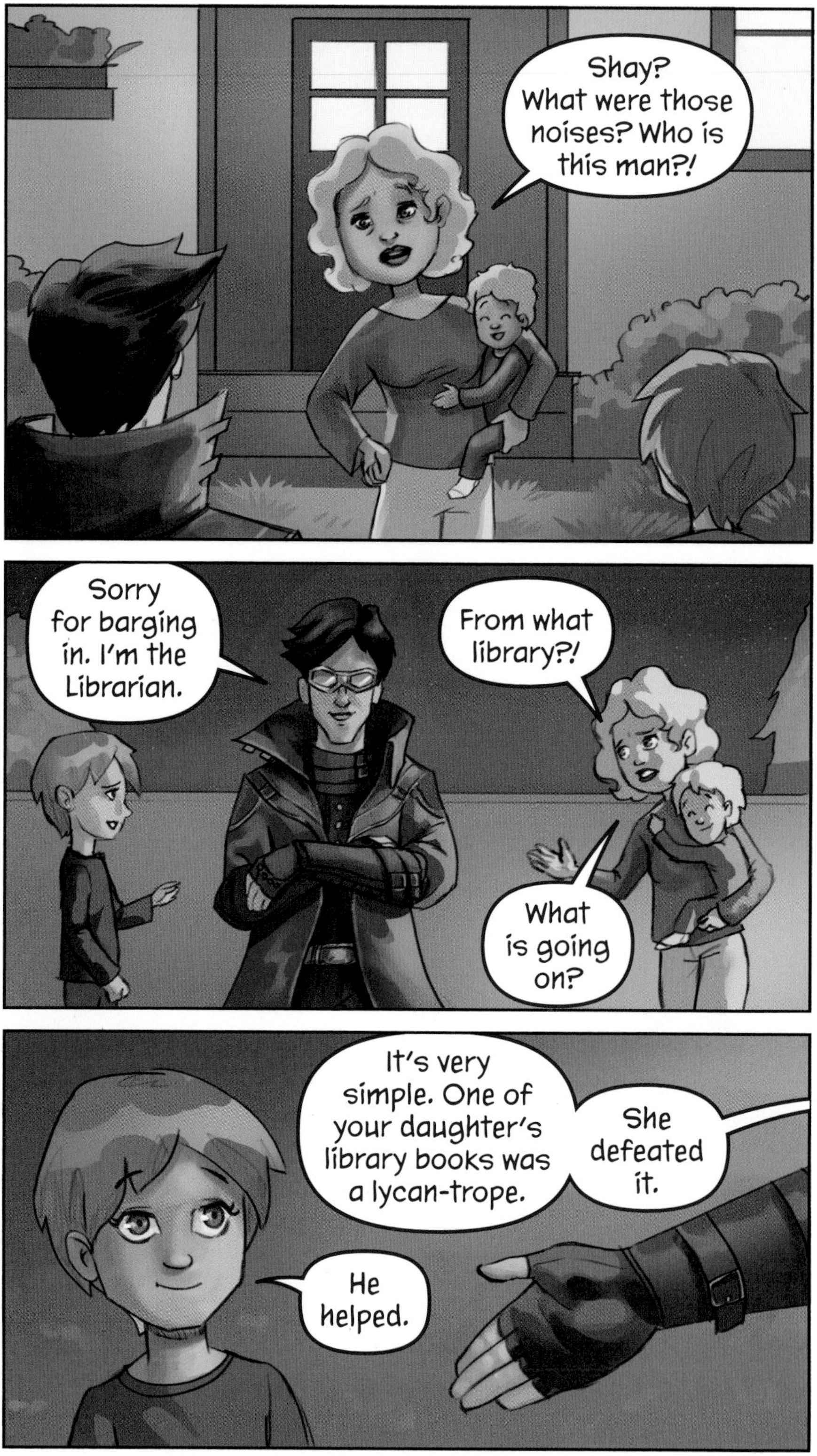
Shay? What were those noises? Who is this man?!
Sorry for barging in. I'm the Librarian.
From what library?!
What is going on?
It's very simple. One of your daughter's library books was a lycan-trope.
She defeated it.
He helped.

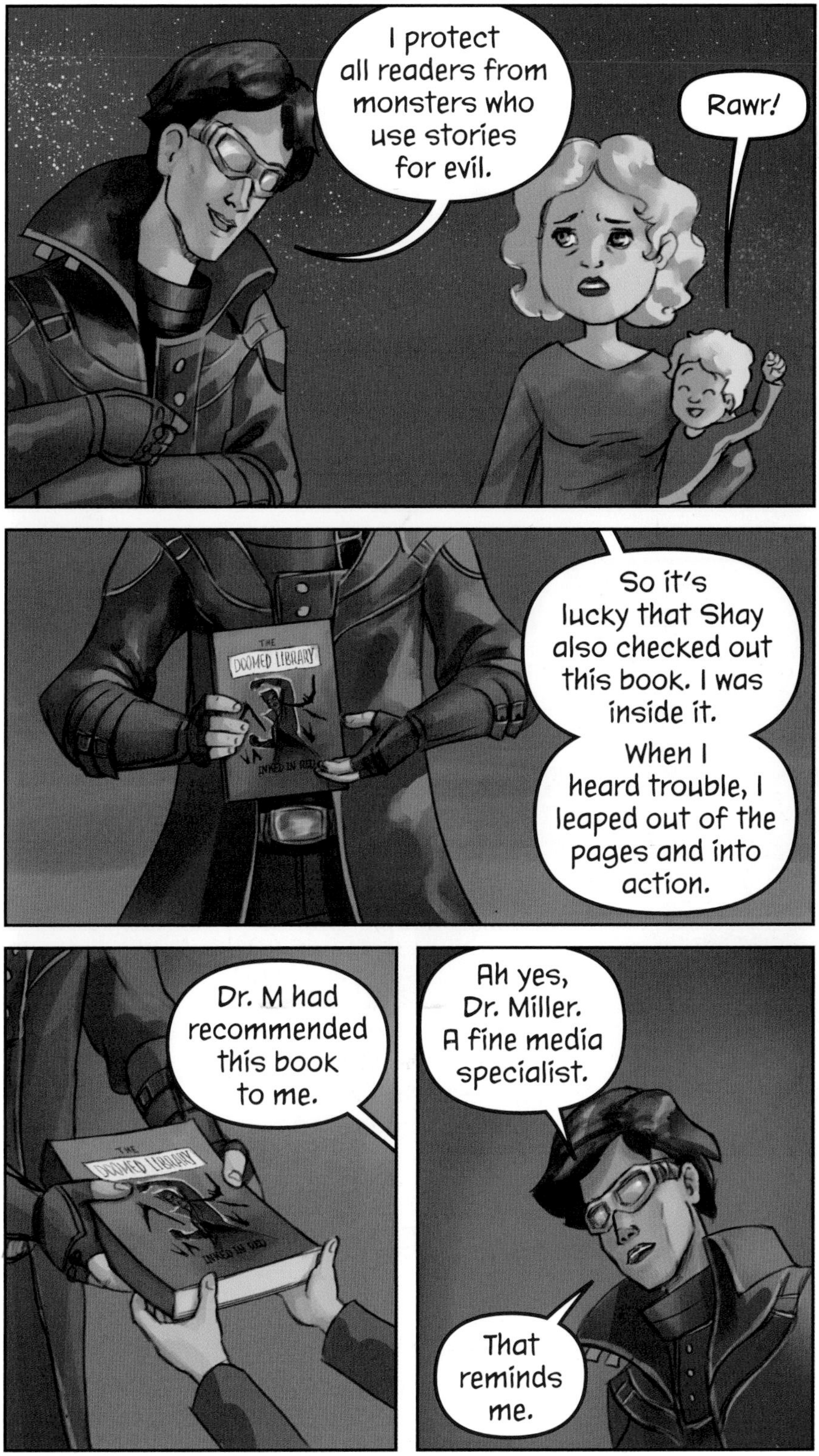
I protect all readers from monsters who use stories for evil.
Rawr!
THE DOOMED LIBRARY
INKED IN RED
So it's lucky that Shay also checked out this book. I was inside it.
When I heard trouble, I leaped out of the pages and into action.
Dr. M had recommended this book to me.
Ah yes, Dr. Miller. A fine media specialist.
That reminds me.

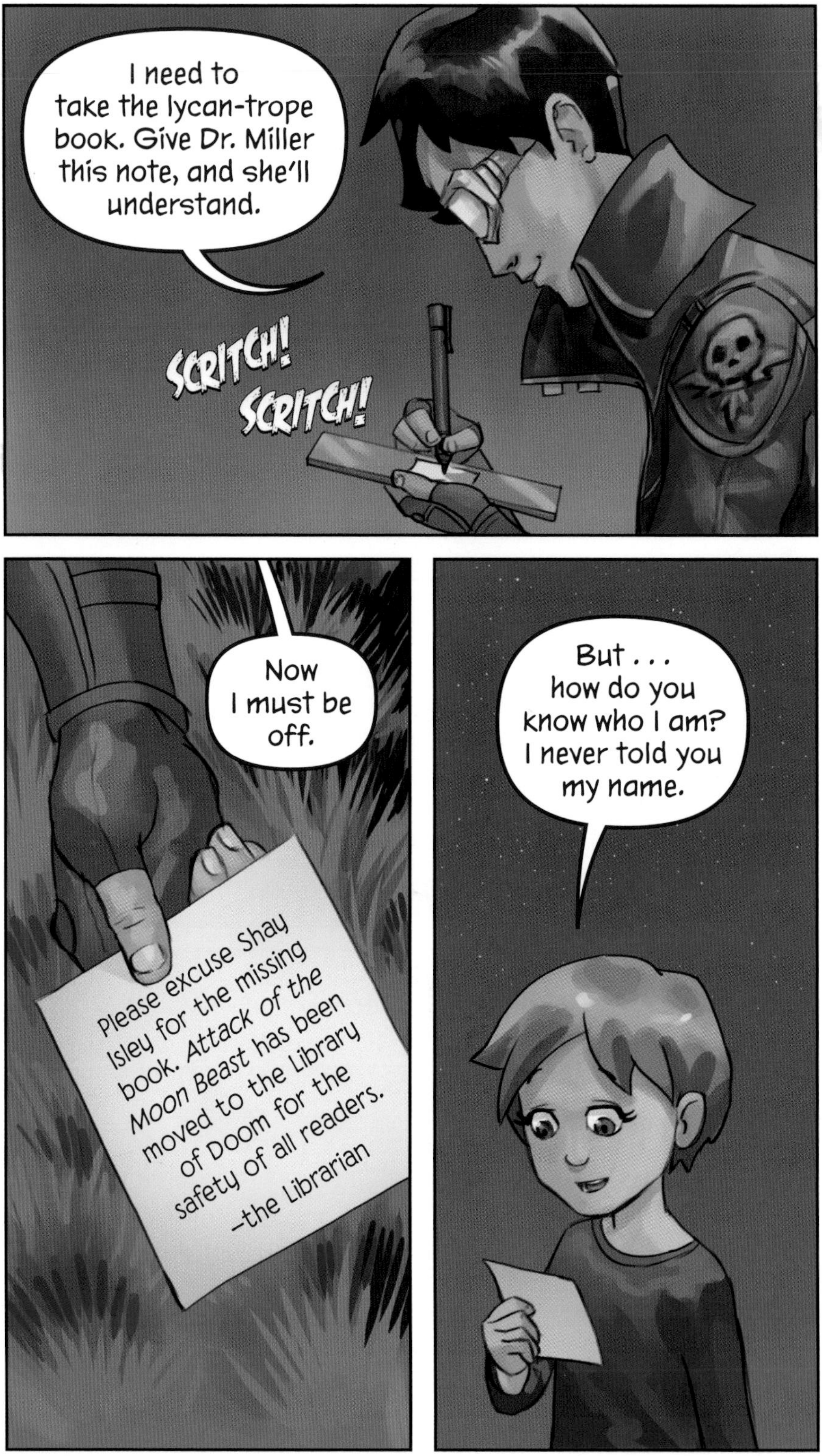
I need to take the lycan-trope book. Give Dr. Miller this note, and she'll understand.
SCRITCH! SCRITCH!
Now I must be off.
Please excuse Shay Isley for the missing book. *Attack of the Moon Beast* has been moved to the Library of Doom for the safety of all readers.
–the Librarian
But . . . how do you know who I am? I never told you my name.

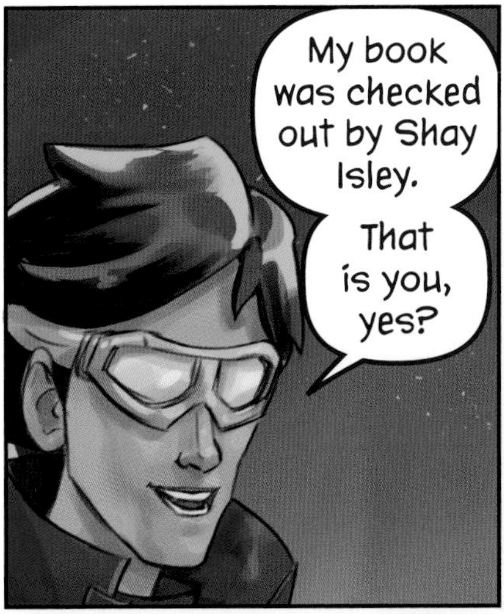
My book was checked out by Shay Isley.
That is you, yes?
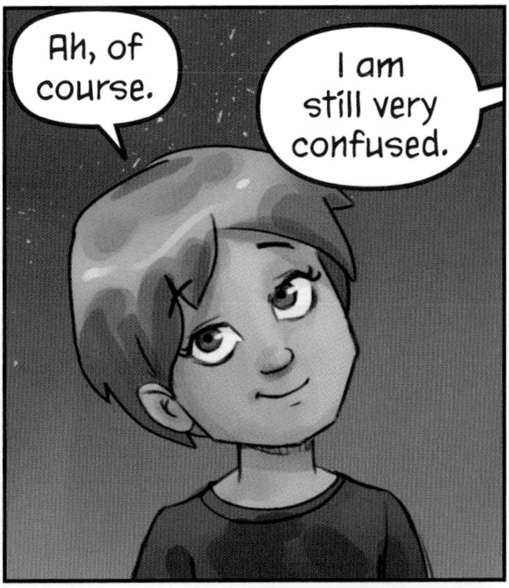
Ah, of course.
I am still very confused.
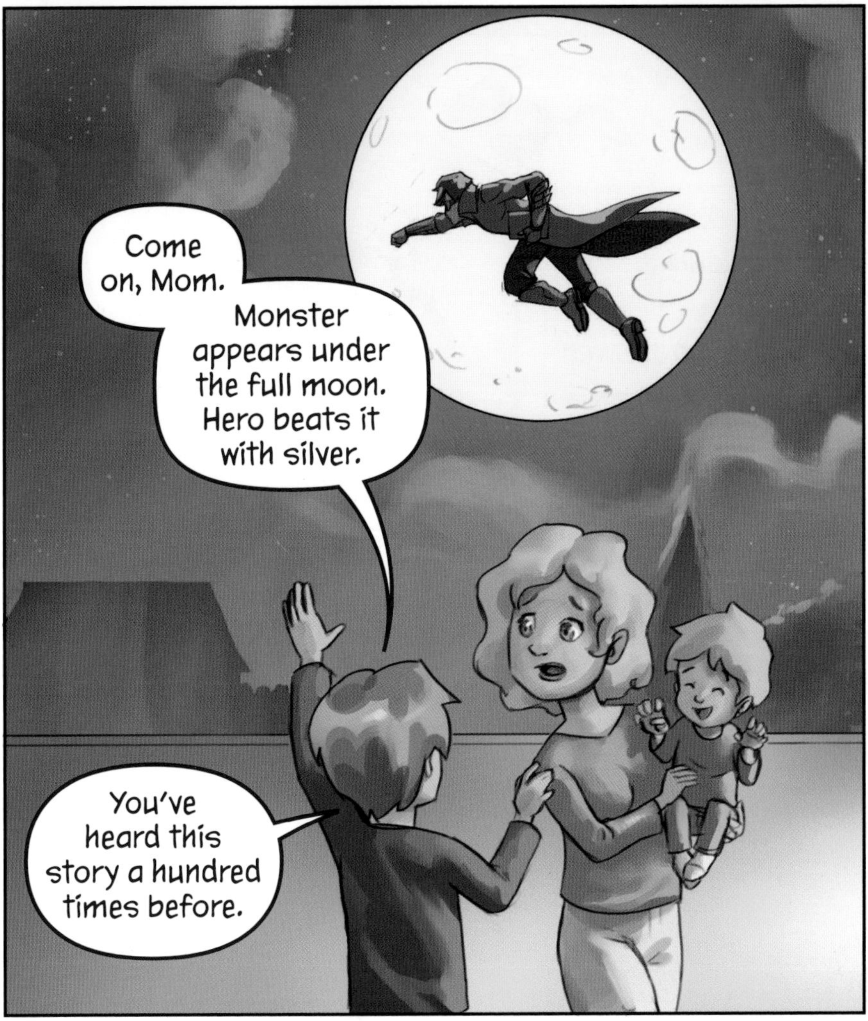
Come on, Mom.
Monster appears under the full moon. Hero beats it with silver.
You've heard this story a hundred times before.

LOOK CLOSER

1

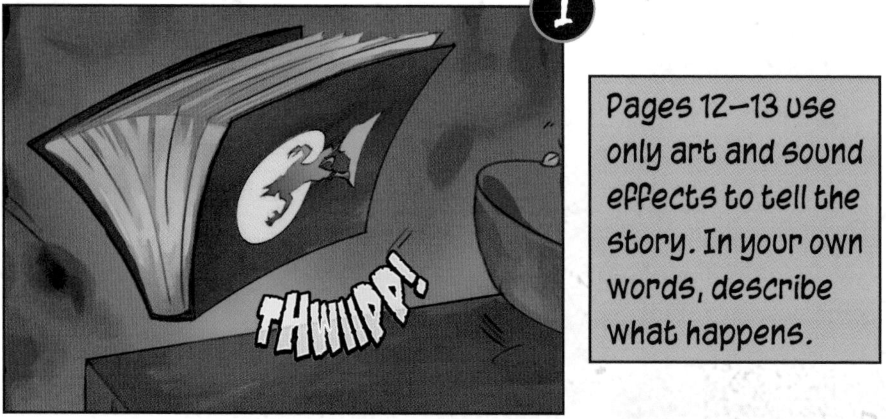
THWIIPP!

Pages 12–13 use only art and sound effects to tell the story. In your own words, describe what happens.

2

How does Shay feel about defeating the beast herself? Support your answer with examples from the art and text.

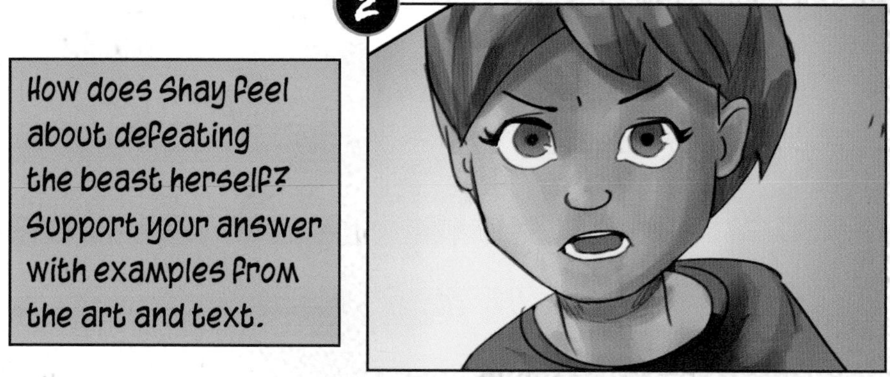

3

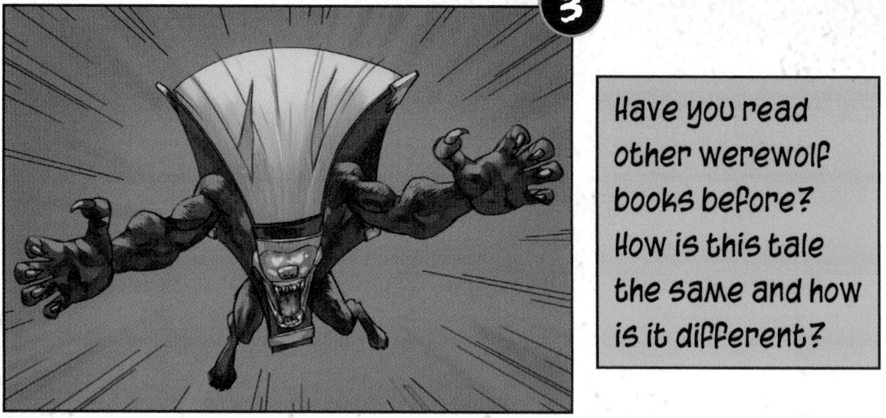

Have you read other werewolf books before? How is this tale the same and how is it different?

GLOSSARY

browse (BROWZ)—to look at many things in order to try to find something you're interested in

cursed (KURSD)—put under an evil spell that is meant to do harm

defeat (dih-FEET)—to beat or overcome someone or something

lycanthrope (LIE-kuhn-throhp)—another term for werewolf; a person who turns into a wolf at night when the moon is full

protect (proh-TEKT)—to keep safe from harm

recommend (reh-kuh-MEND)—to say something is good and should be chosen

thrill (THRIL)—a feeling of great happiness and excitement

trope (TROHP)—a common or overused theme in books, movies, and other types of stories

ABOUT THE WRITER

STEVE BREZENOFF is the author of more than fifty middle-grade chapter books, including the series Field Trip Mysteries, Ravens Pass, and Return to Titanic. He has also written three young adult novels, *Guy in Real Life*; *Brooklyn, Burning*; and *The Absolute Value of -1*. In his spare time, he enjoys video games, cycling, and cooking. Steve lives in Minneapolis with his wife, Beth, and their son and daughter.

ABOUT THE ARTIST

IANIO GARCIA has been working as an illustrator and concept artist since 2012 for magazines, books, movies, and games. He loves digital painting, podcasts, and coffee. You can find out more about him by searching in some hidden part of the Library of Doom.

AN M. NIGHT SHYAMALAN FILM

THE LAST AIRBENDER

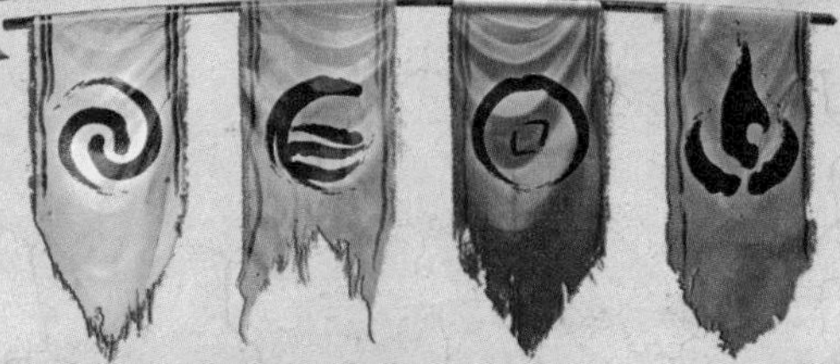

AANG'S DESTINY

by Emily Sollinger

based on the series *Avatar: The Last Airbender*

created by Michael Dante DiMartino and Bryan Konietzko

based on the screenplay written by M. Night Shyamalan

Simon Spotlight
New York London Toronto Sydney

SIMON SPOTLIGHT

An imprint of Simon & Schuster Children's Publishing Division

1230 Avenue of the Americas, New York, New York 10020

© 2010 by Paramount Pictures. All Rights Reserved. *The Last Airbender* and all related titles,
logos, and characters are trademarks of Viacom International Inc.

All rights reserved, including the right of reproduction in whole or in part in any form.

SIMON SPOTLIGHT, READY-TO-READ, and colophon are registered trademarks of Simon & Schuster, Inc.

For information about special discounts for bulk purchases, please contact Simon & Schuster Special Sales
at 1-866-506-1949 or business@simonandschuster.com.

Manufactured in the United States of America 0410 LAK

First Edition 10 9 8 7 6 5 4 3 2 1

Library of Congress Cataloging-in-Publication Data

Sollinger, Emily.

Aang's destiny / by Emily Sollinger ; based on the screenplay by M. Night Shyamalan. —w 1st ed.

p. cm. — (Ready-to-read)

"The Last Airbender."

ISBN 978-1-4169-9938-6

I. Shyamalan, M. Night. II. Last airbender (Motion picture) III. Title.

PZ7.S6953Aan 2010

[E]—dc22

2010000498

CHAPTER 1

On a vast icy plain under a cold gray sky, a boy was slowly waking up. Shards of broken ice lay around him as a large creature slept beside him. Katara, a girl from the Water Tribe, and her brother, Sokka, tried to help the boy.

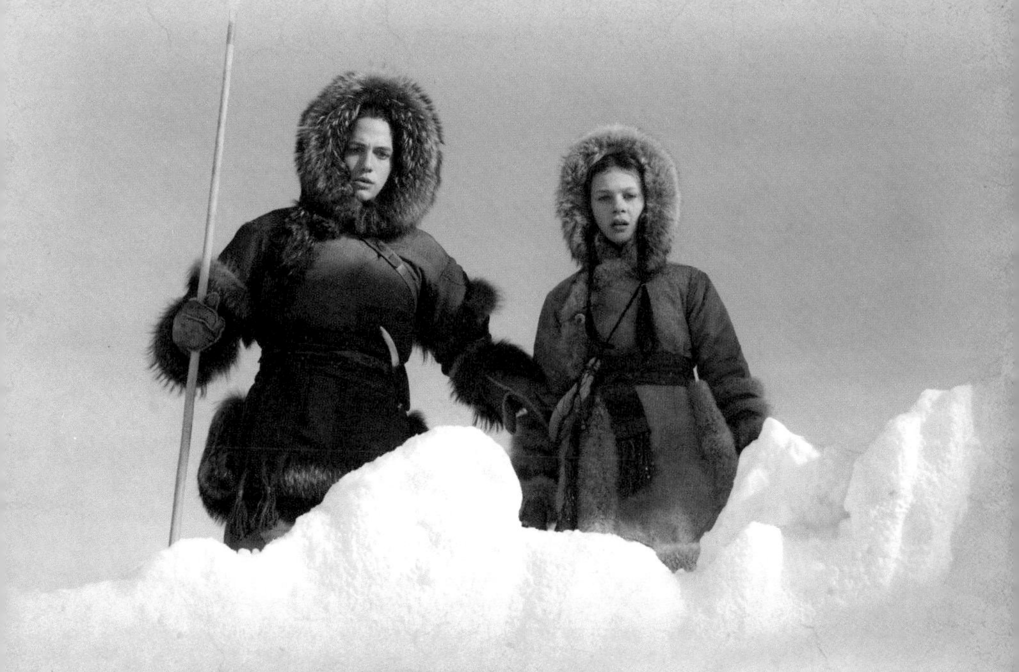

"What's your name?" Katara asked. The boy looked back at her weakly—and fainted.

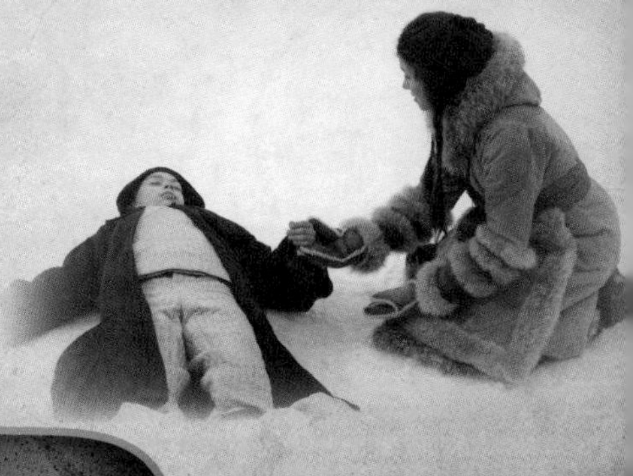

Katara and Sokka carefully carried the boy back to their village so he could rest.

When the boy awoke, Katara had many questions for him.

"How did you get all the way out here?" she asked.

"I ran away from home. It wasn't smart, but I was upset," the boy replied.

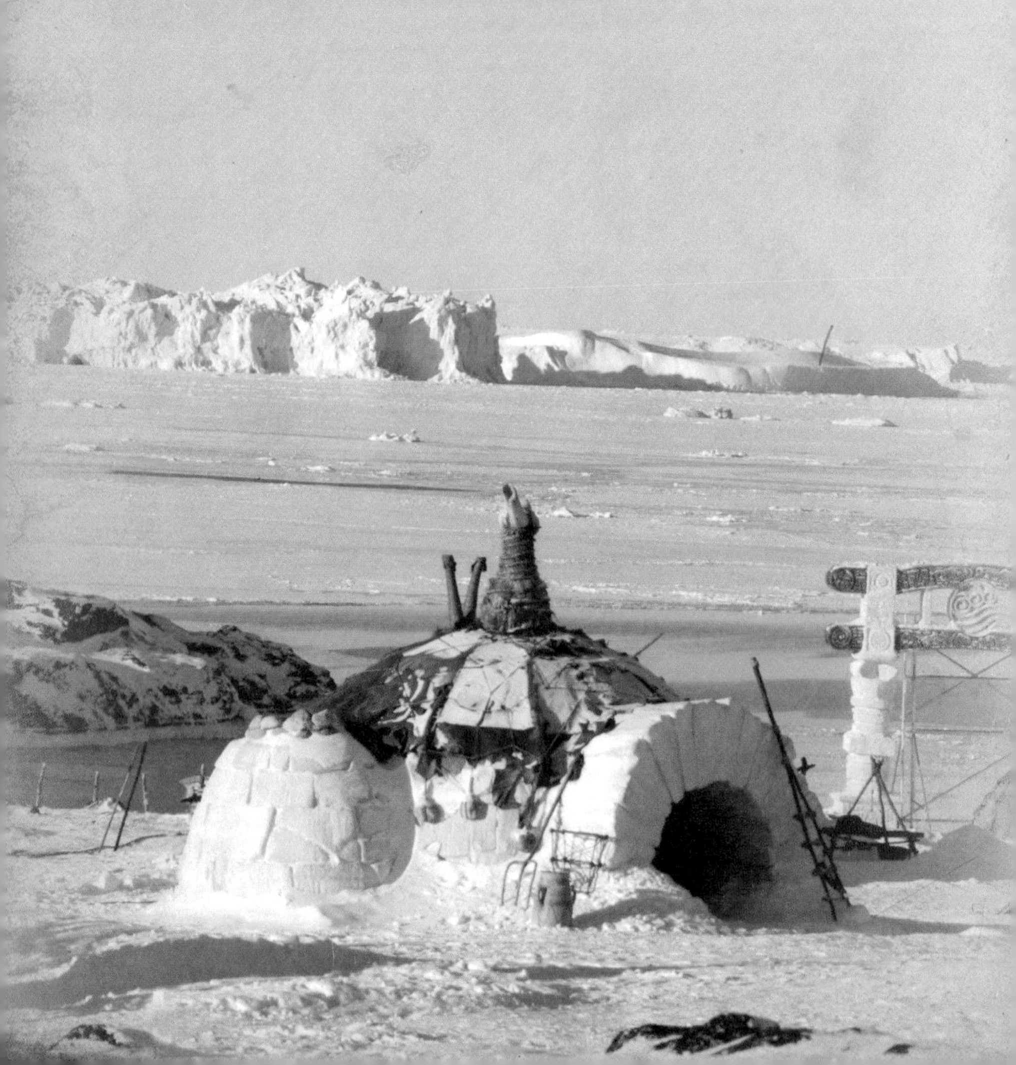

"I get like that too," Katara said.

The boy smiled. "Thanks for saving me."

"You are welcome," Katara said, then added, "Oh, and your animal . . ."

"His name is Appa," explained the boy.

"He's fine. He's near the stream at the edge of our village," said Katara.

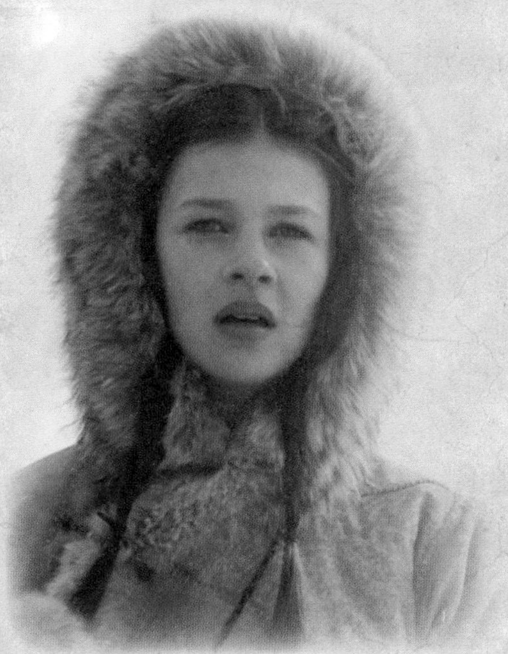

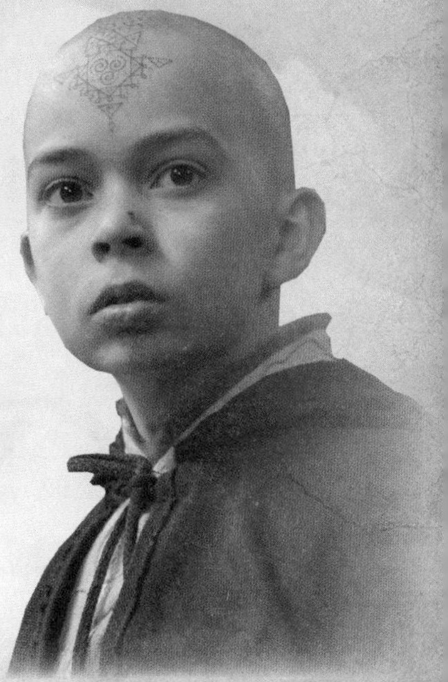

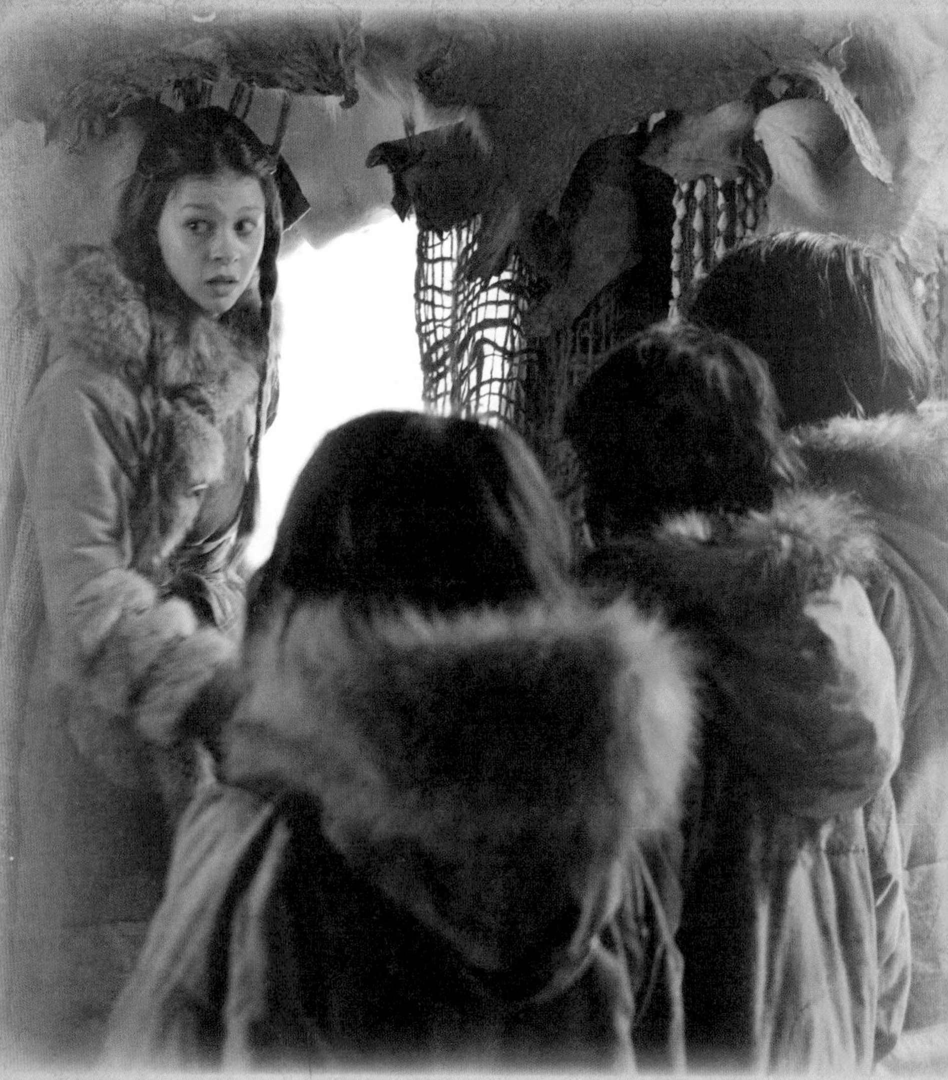

“I should probably get going,” the boy said. “They will all be worried about me back at home.”

“You’re not still upset?” Katara asked.

“Not as much as I was,” the boy replied.

CHAPTER TWO

Creak, crackle . . . shatter!

The loud sound of something breaking startled Sokka, and he rushed to see what it was. A large ship had broken the ice and was pushing its way through!

Sokka warned everyone, "The Fire Nation is here! Don't come out until I tell you it's safe."

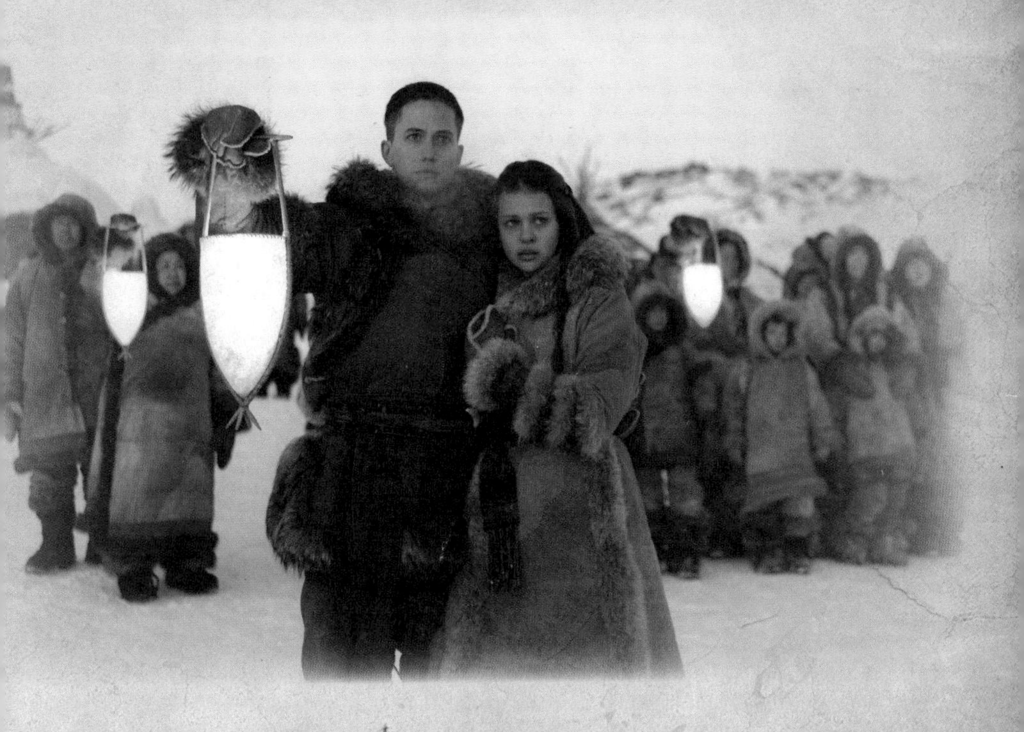

The Fire Nation soldiers marched through the village. They were led by a young man barking orders.

"I am Prince Zuko, son of Fire Lord Ozai and heir to the Fire Nation throne," he declared.

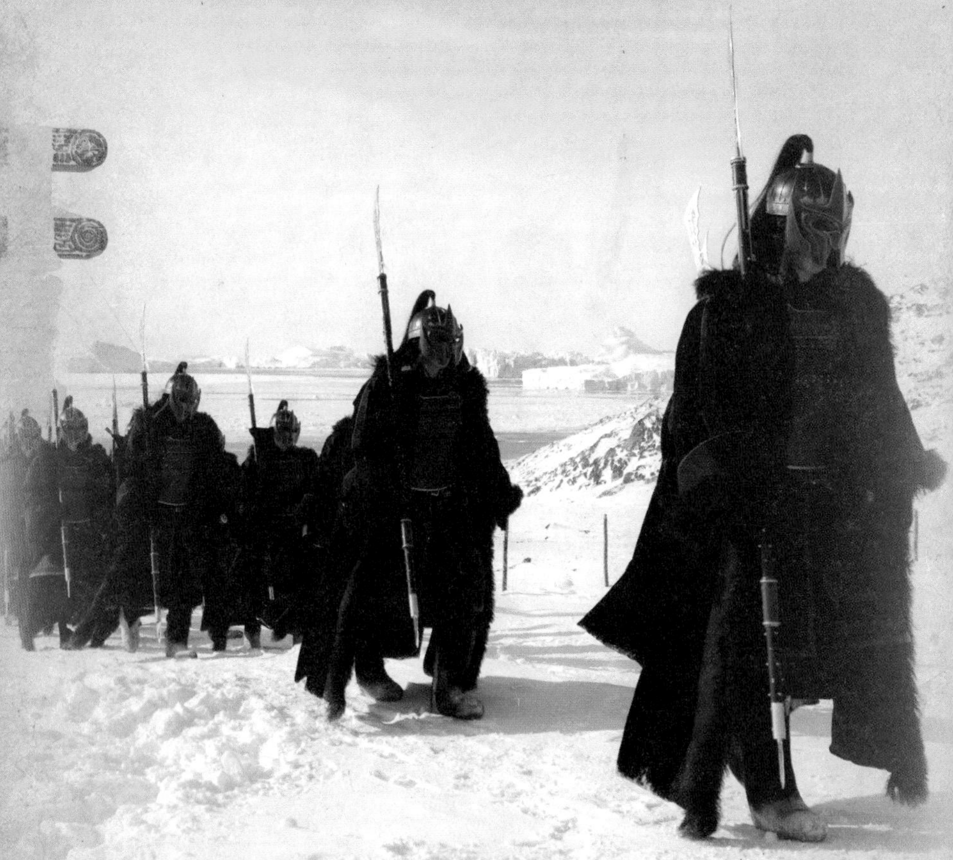

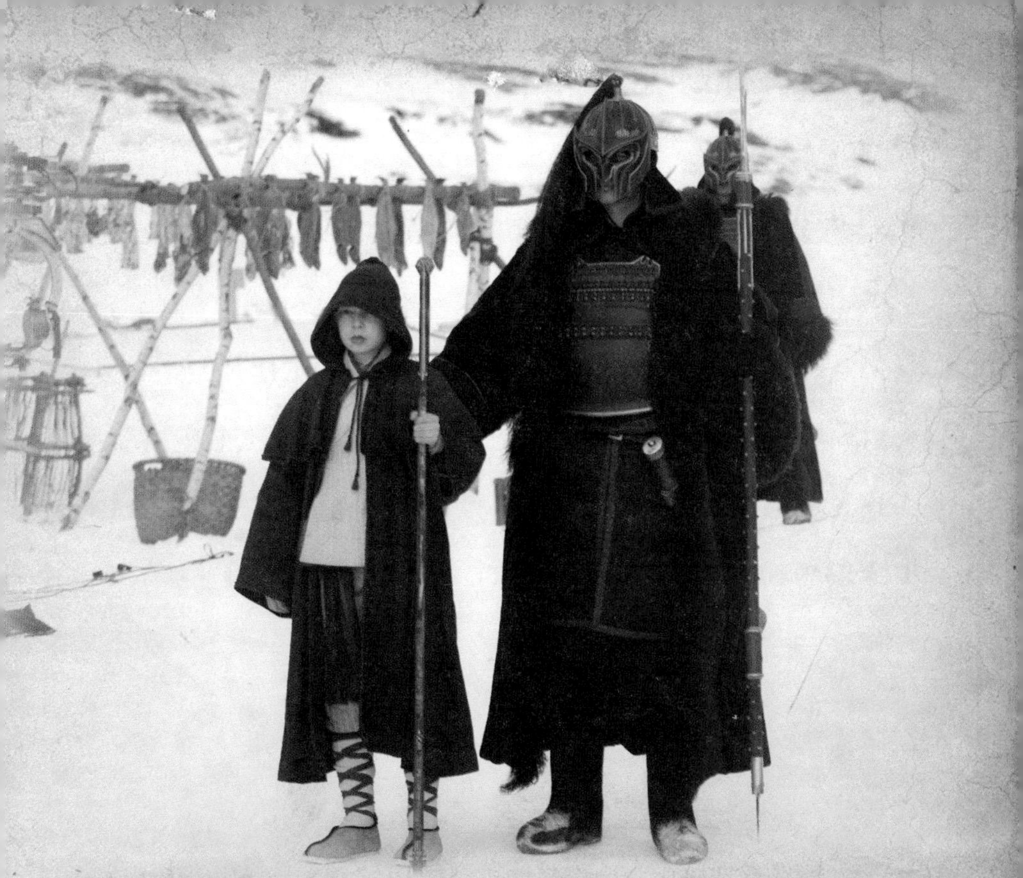

The prince ordered his soldiers to bring him the boy Katara and Sokka had found.

"Who are you? What's your name?" he asked.

"I don't need to tell you anything," the boy replied.

"Come with me to my ship! If you don't, I will destroy this village."

"I'll go with you," said the boy. "Just don't hurt anyone."

When the boy boarded the ship with Prince Zuko, he was met by an older man.

"What do you want with me?" the boy asked.

"My name is Iroh," the man said kindly. "My nephew wants me to perform a test on you. It will only take a few moments. Then you are free to go."

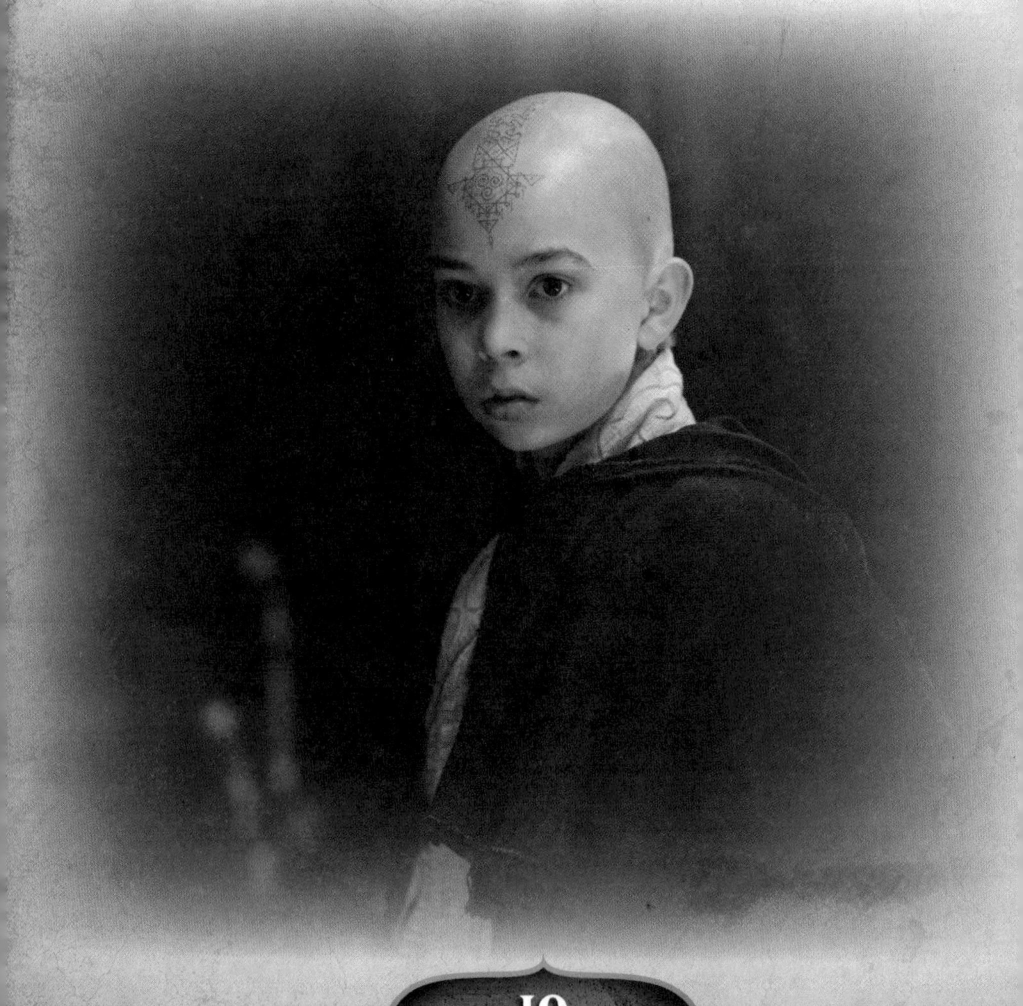

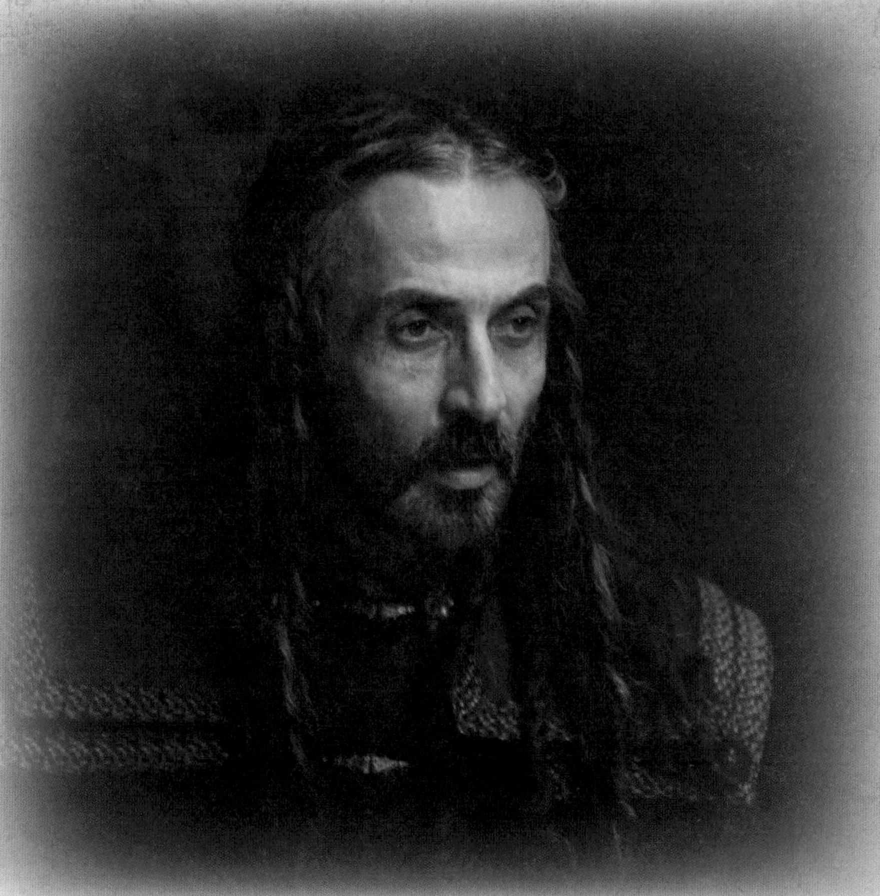

Iroh led the boy to a small table and put a tray of objects in front of him. He lit a candle and pushed it toward the boy. The flickering flame became completely still.

Next Iroh poured water from a small jug onto the table. The water formed a perfect circle in front of the boy. Finally Iroh took out a rock—and it balanced on one end!

Suddenly Prince Zuko shouted, "You are my prisoner! I'm taking you back to the Fire Nation."

The confused boy looked at Iroh.

But Iroh shook his head. "I'm sorry. I should have explained myself better. If you failed the test, you were free to leave. As it turns out, you are the only one in the entire world who could have passed this test."

Then he added, "It is truly an honor to be in your presence."

The boy knew he needed to get out quickly.

"Don't even try to escape!" Prince Zuko yelled. "This room is made entirely of metal, there are guards everywhere, and my uncle and I are expert firebenders."

But the boy was not afraid. Gathering all his strength, he pushed himself away from the table.

Then he brought his hands together and sent a huge gust of wind forward—pushing himself out the door, and slamming it closed.

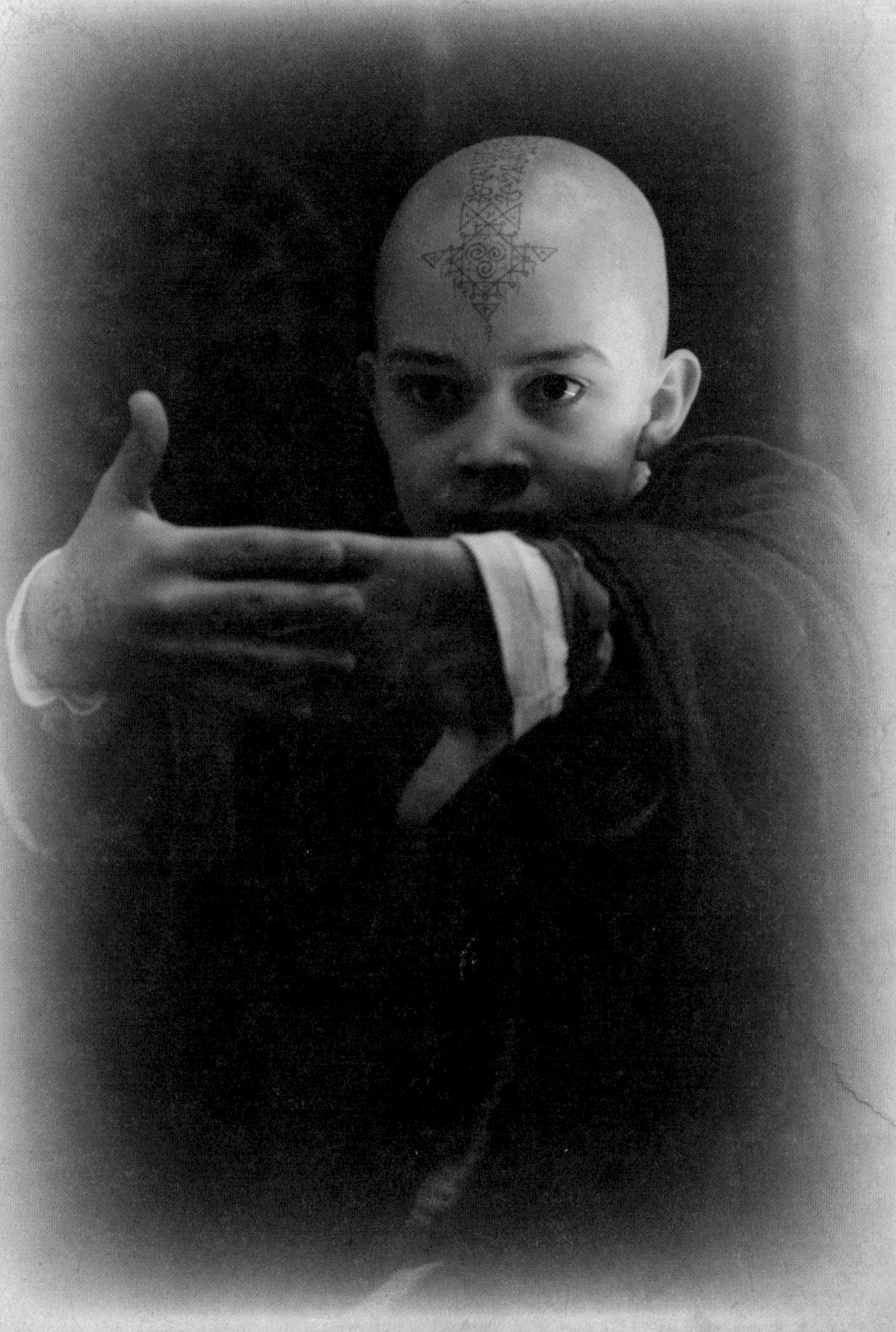

CHAPTER THREE

Meanwhile, back in the village, Sokka and Katara were waiting anxiously.

"If I ever see that Prince Zuko again, he and I are going to have a real problem!" Katara said. "He walked around like he owned our village. We have to stand up to him! We have to save that boy!"

"They're on a huge ship," Sokka said. "They are miles away by now. How could we ever catch up?"

Just then they heard children giggling and playing. When they stepped outside, they were awestruck. Appa was floating in the air while the little ones were laughing as they hung on to his feet and tail.

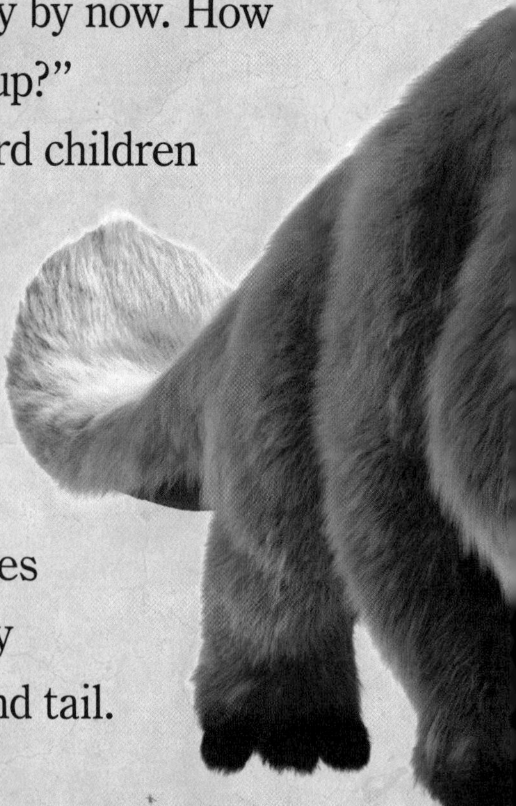

Sokka and Katara looked at each other.

"Now that could probably catch the ship," Sokka said.

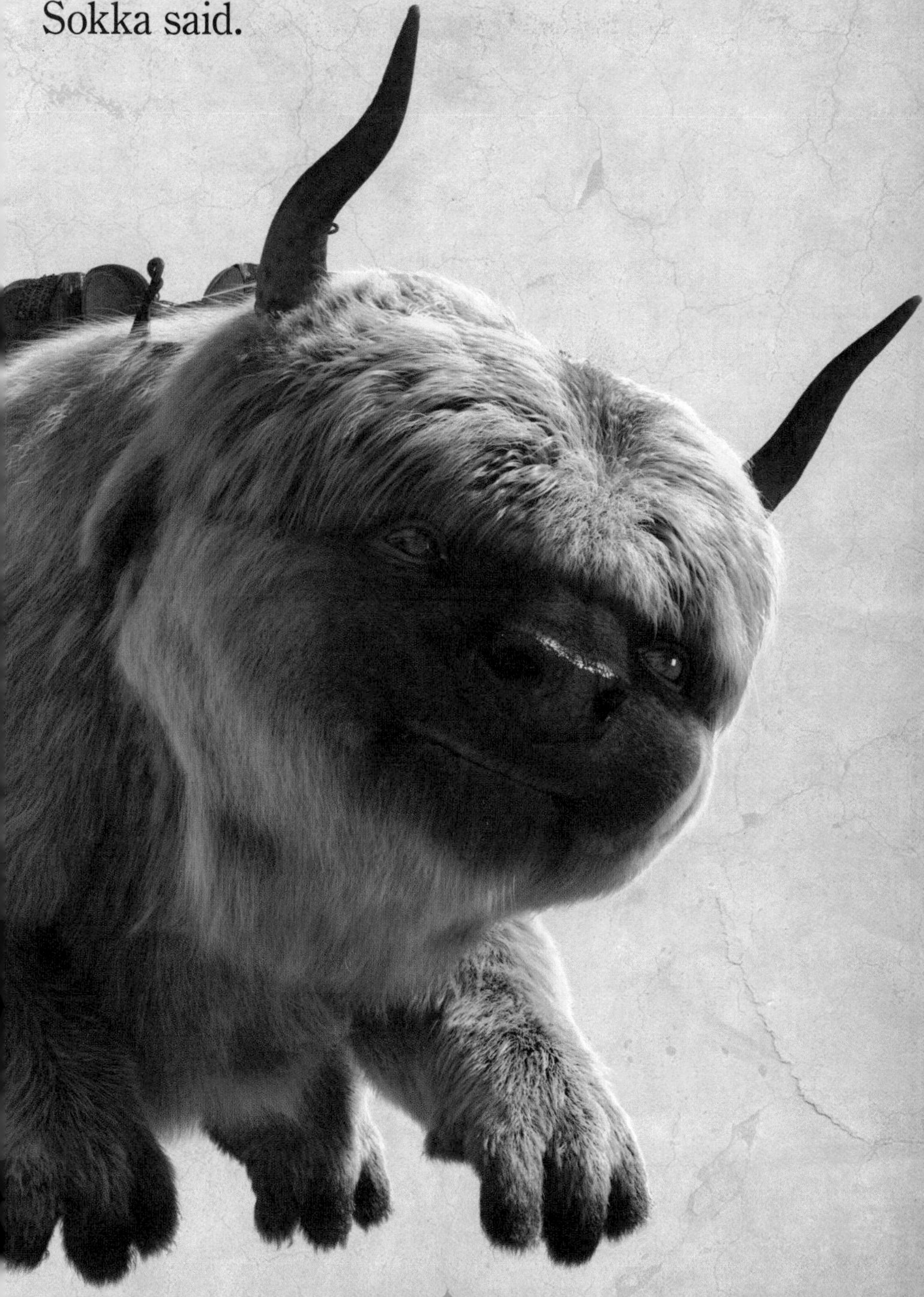

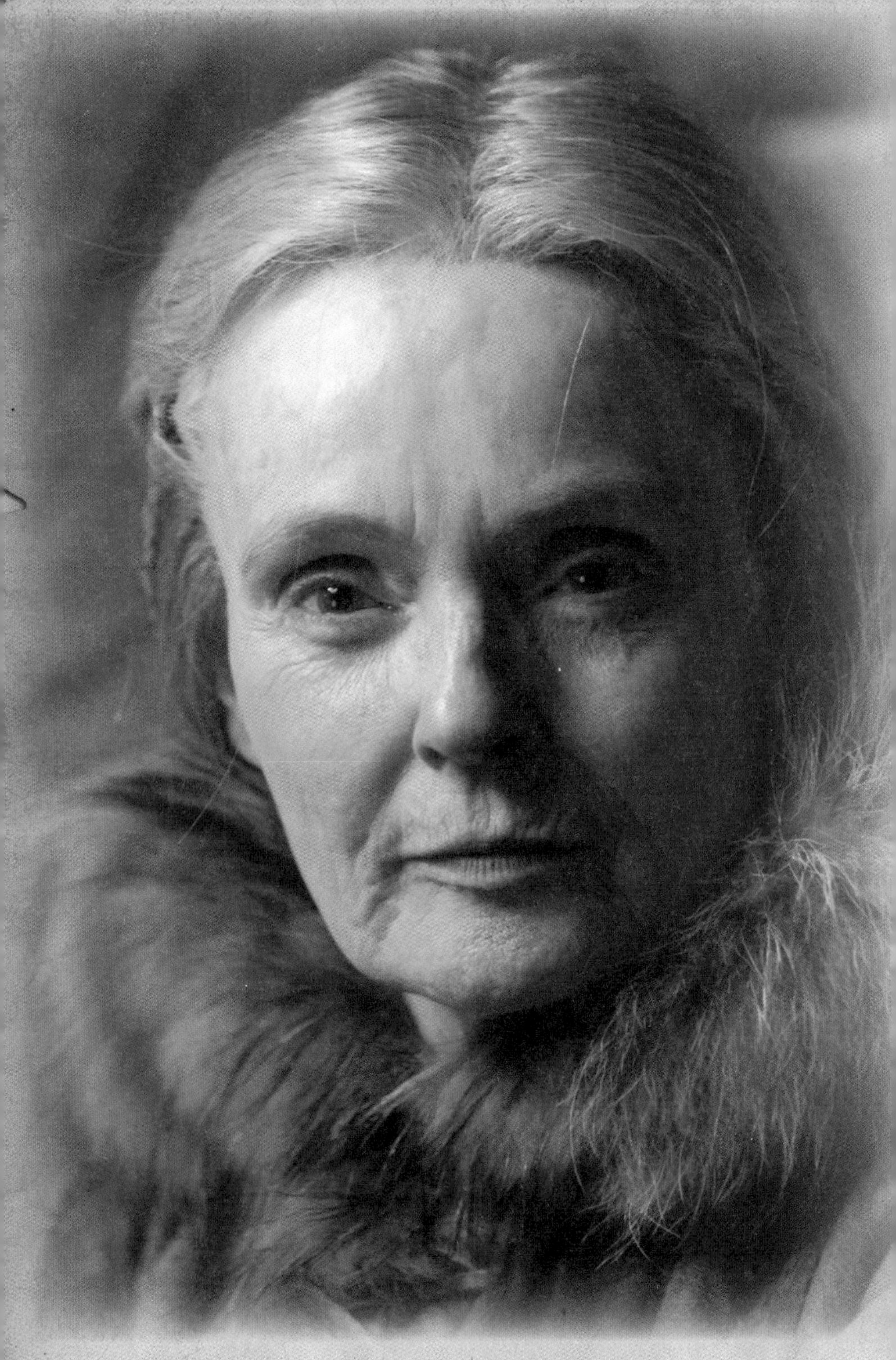

As Sokka and Katara gathered supplies for their trip, their grandmother watched quietly.

"Are you going to try to stop us, Grandma?" Katara asked.

Grandma asked Katara and Sokka to sit down. "Katara, I knew that from the moment we discovered you were a waterbender, we would one day learn your destiny," she said.

"Did you see that boy's tattoos? Tattoos like that haven't been seen in almost a century. I think they are airbending tattoos. Children . . . I think you may have found the Avatar."

Katara and Sokka couldn't believe it! The Avatar was the only person who could stop the Fire Nation and bring peace to the world.

"I believe your destinies are tied," Grandma continued. "You found him. He will need the two of you, and we all need him. You are about to go on a great adventure. Just promise me that you will come back to me safely."

"We promise, Grandma," answered Sokka and Katara as they hugged her.

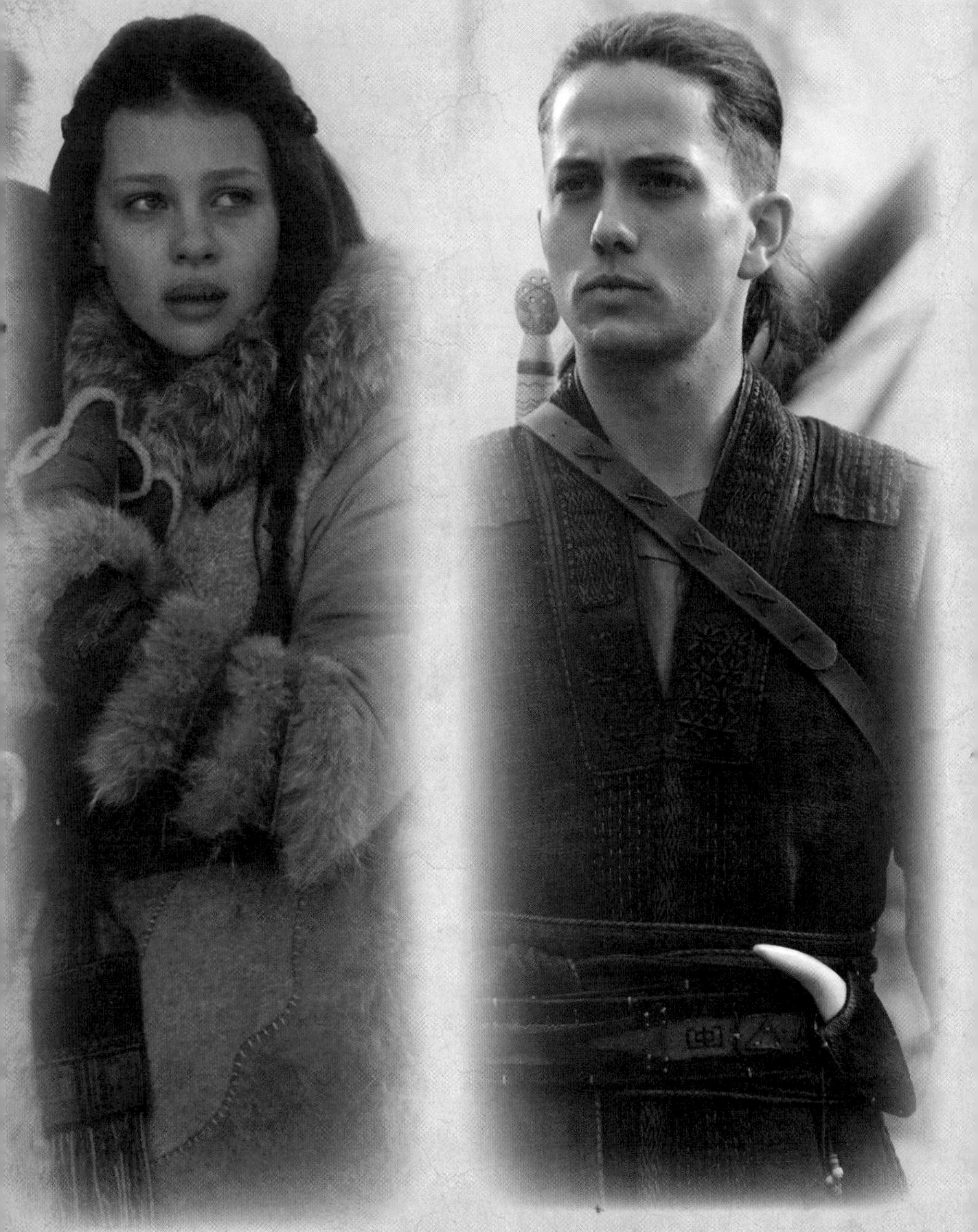

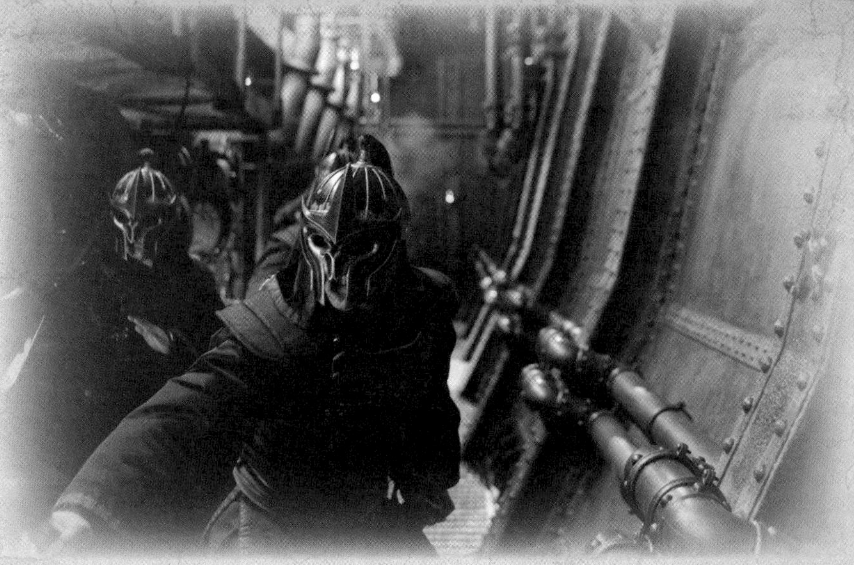

The boy escaped from Prince Zuko and ran to the deck of the ship.

Fire Nation guards were now chasing him, and he was just out of luck.

"Don't move," Prince Zuko ordered sternly. "You have nowhere to run."

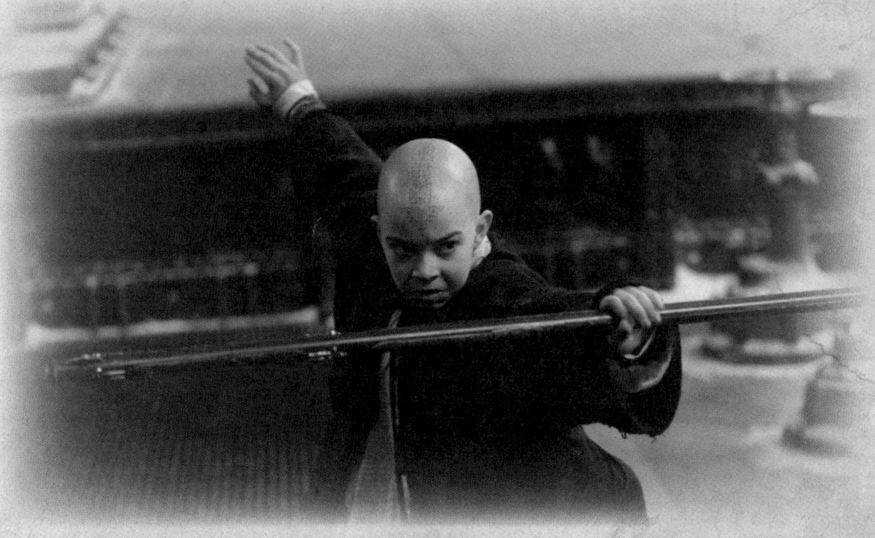

Just then the boy heard the wailing of an animal. He looked out beyond the ship and saw Appa floating high above an ice ridge! Katara and Sokka were seated on Appa's back.

The boy shook his staff so that wings appeared on each side of the stick. Then he glided right up to Appa.

"You came just in time," the boy told his new friends.

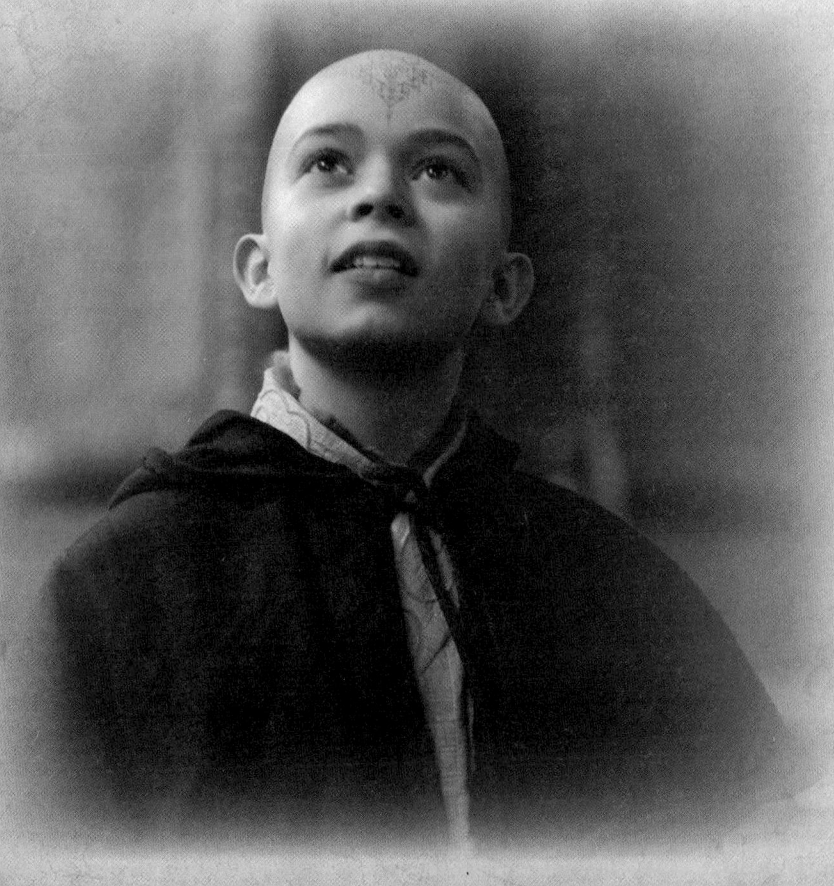

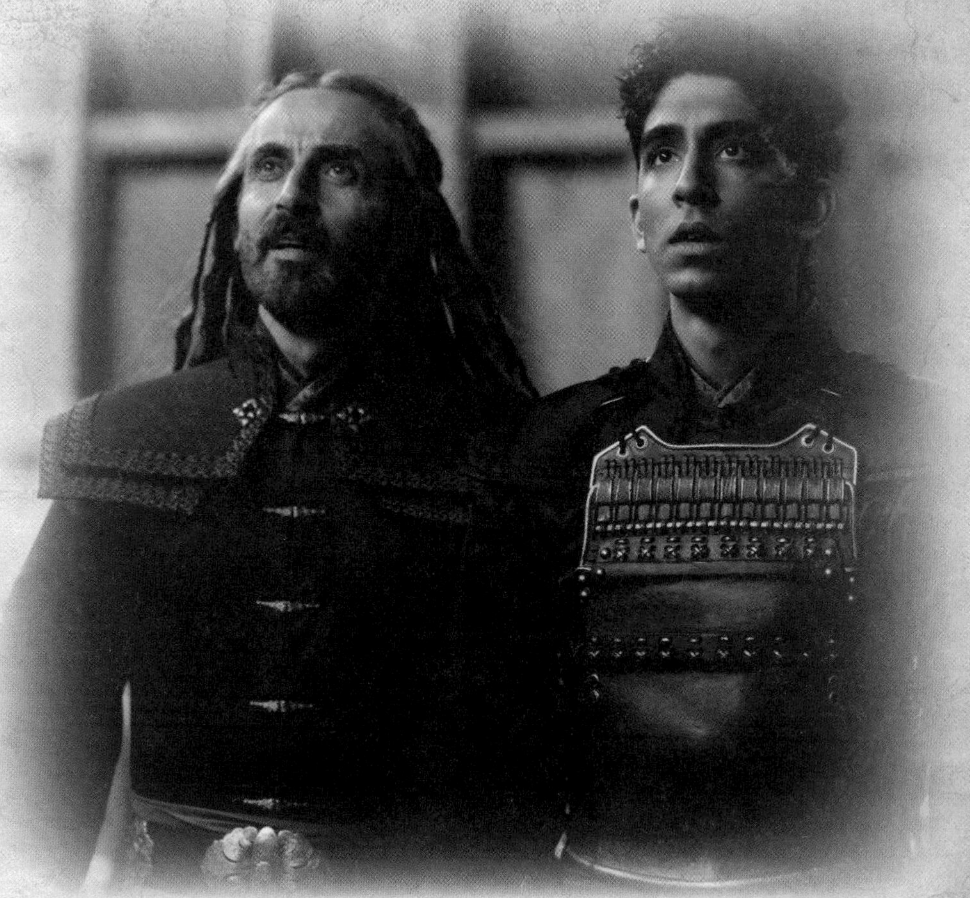

Prince Zuko and his Uncle Iroh watched as Appa carried the Avatar away.

"You found the Avatar!" said Iroh. "People have been searching for him for generations, and you found him. It's not by chance. Your destinies are tied, Zuko. But one question remains: Where has he been for a hundred years?"

CHAPTER FOUR

"Grandma was right. You can bend air," Sokka said to the boy. "How do you do that?"

"We learn to feel the energy behind the wind—not just the breeze on our skin," explained the boy. Then he added, "The Fire Nation is up to something. I need to go home to figure out what they are planning."

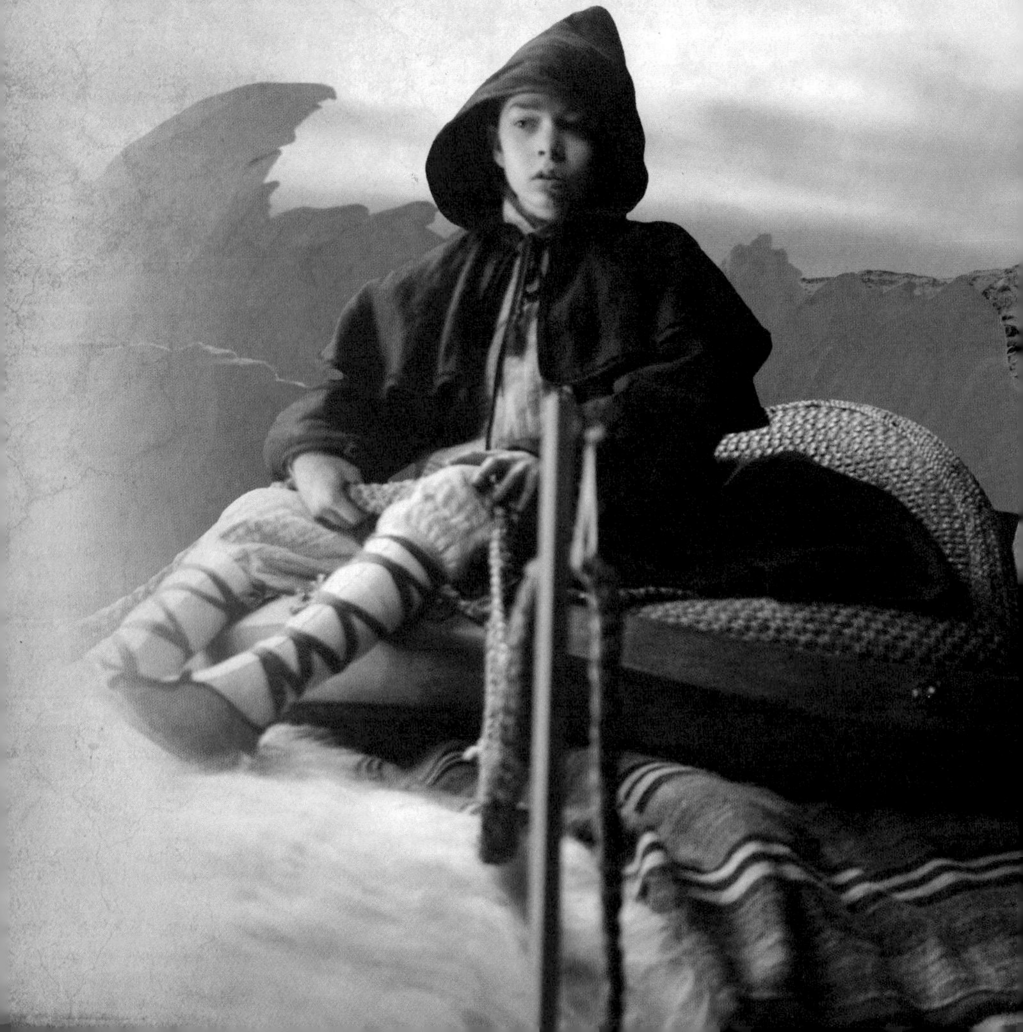

It was dusk when the group landed on a mountaintop.

Climbing down from Appa's back, they found themselves looking at a beautiful temple that was built into the side of the mountain. They had reached the Northern Air Temple.

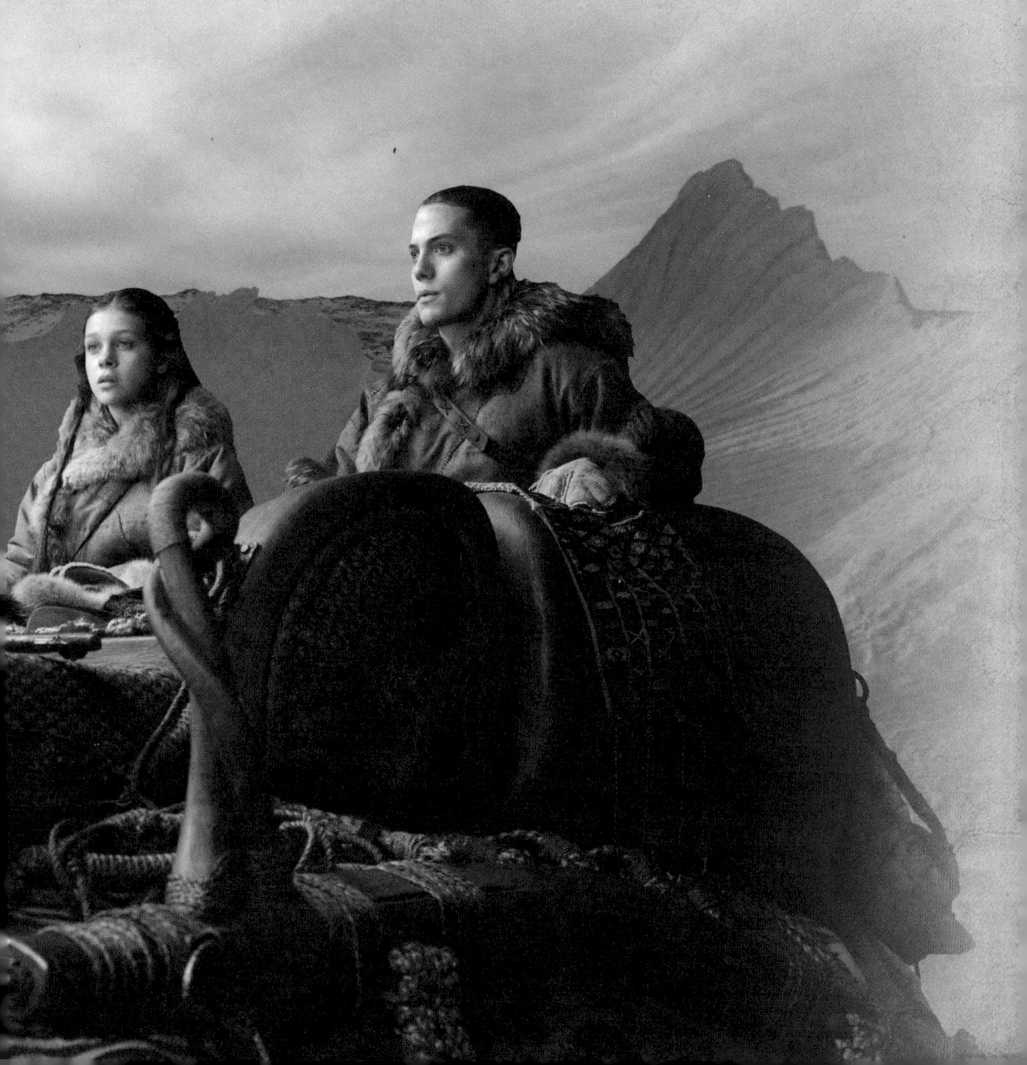

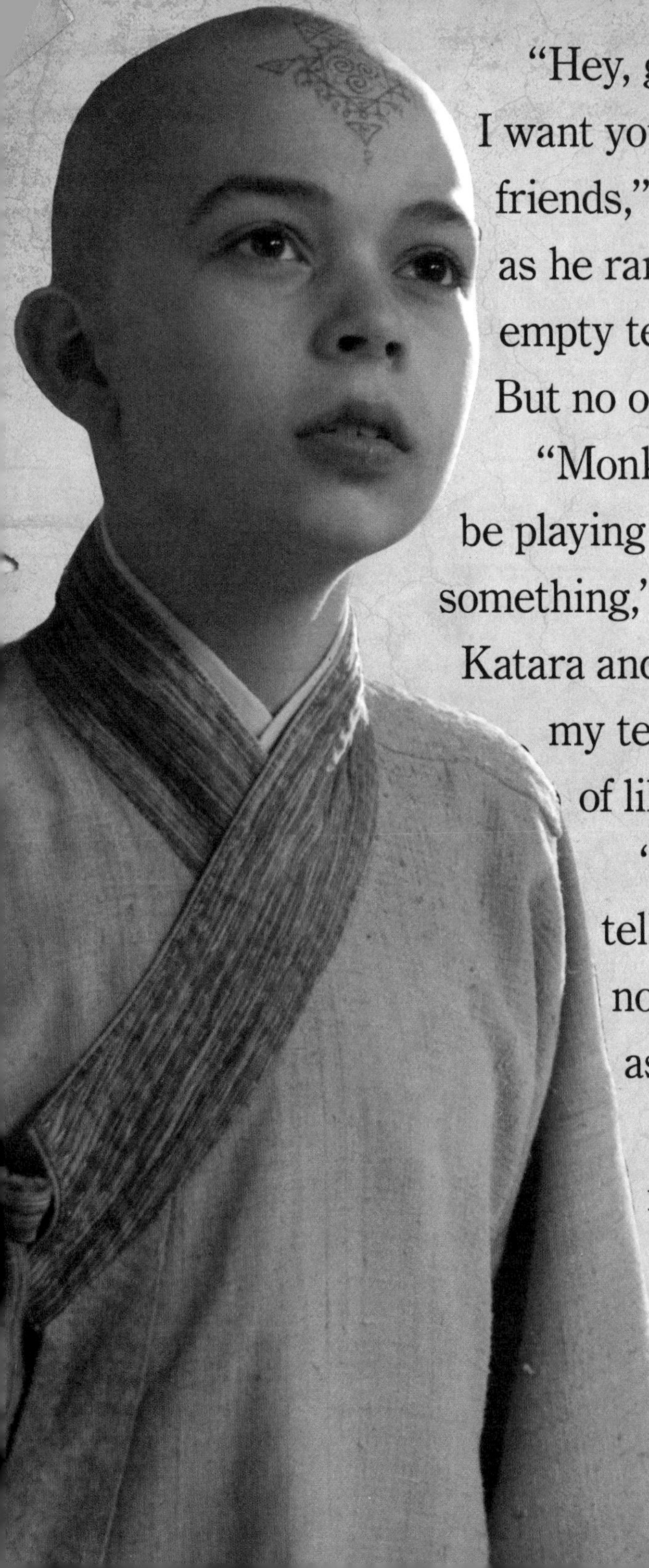

"Hey, guys, I'm back! I want you to meet some friends," the boy called as he ran through an empty temple courtyard. But no one answered.

"Monk Gyatso must be playing a trick or something," the boy told Katara and Sokka. "He's my teacher . . . and kind of like my father."

"Is it okay if you tell me your name now?" Katara asked.

"The monks named me Aang," said the boy.

Aang looked everywhere for the monks.

"Okay, guys, enough!" he shouted.

Just then a noise startled Sokka. "It's a spider-rat!" he cried out. "They're poisonous!"

"He's a flying lemur-bat," Aang corrected. "We keep them as pets."

"Aren't they extinct?" Katara asked.

"Extinct? There must be thousands of them on this mountain."

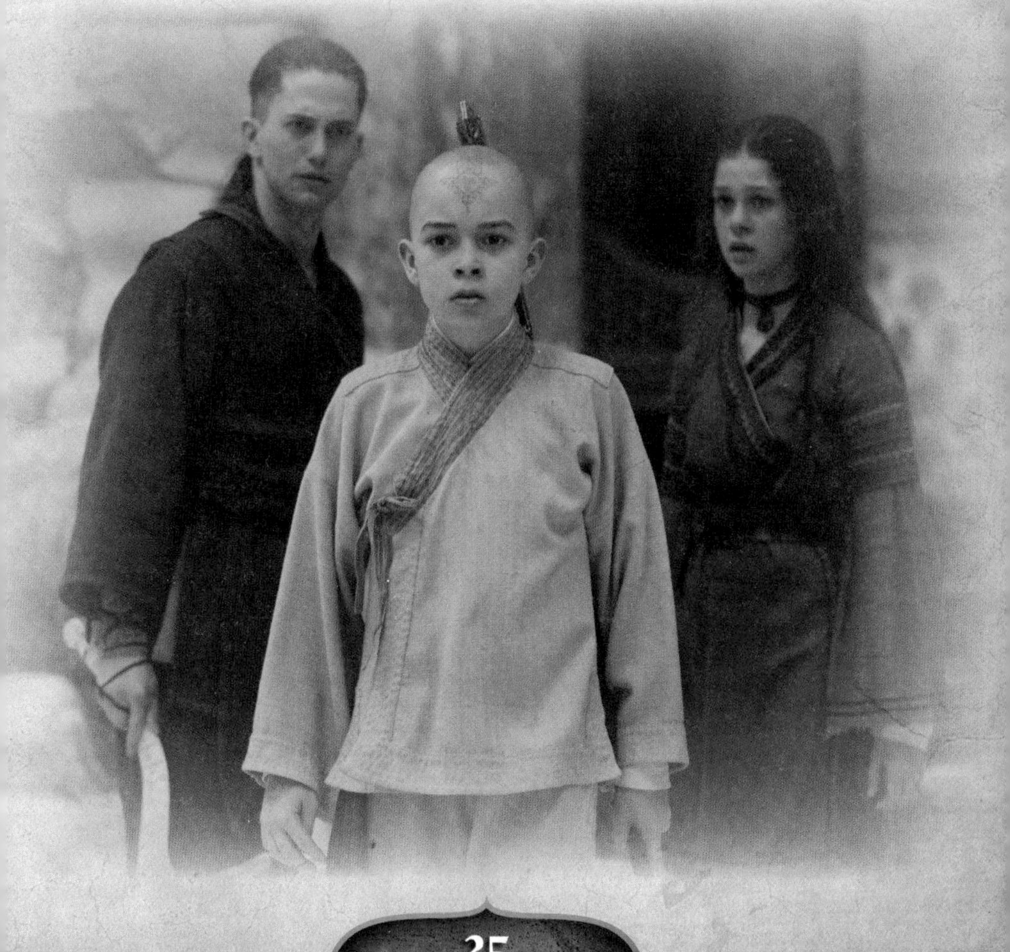

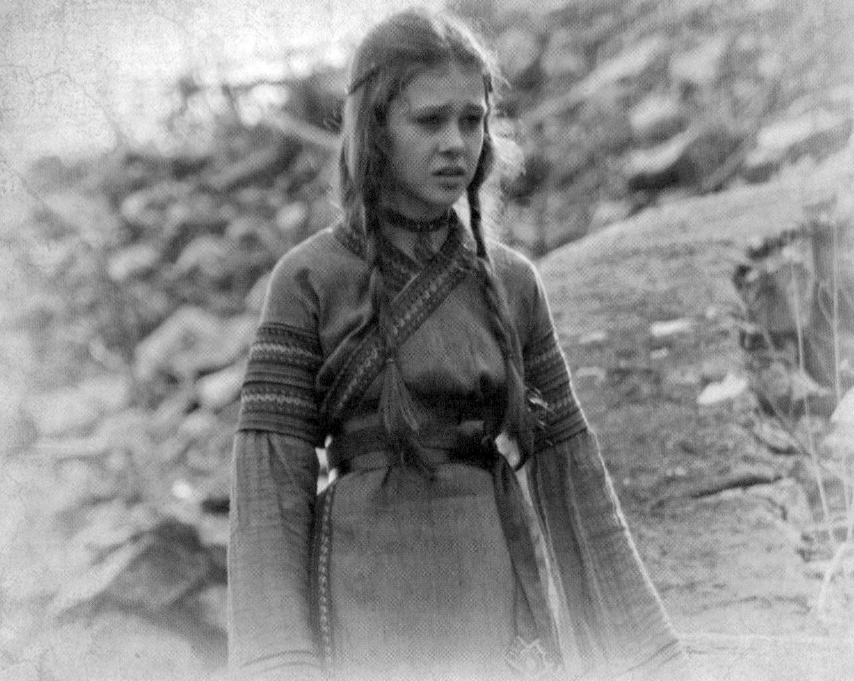

Slowly Katara began to realize the truth about Aang. "Your friends were monks?" she asked.

"Oh, right!" Aang suddenly shouted. "They must be in the prayer field now."

Katara tried to stop Aang, but he was already at the huge field, standing and staring at what lay before him: the remains of an ancient war, with old parts and pieces of Air Nomad and Fire Nation equipment scattered on the ground.

"Aang, I think you were in that ice for almost one hundred years," Katara said.

"But I only left a few days ago," replied Aang.

"The firebenders started a war," she began to gently explain. "They knew that the next Avatar would be an Air Nomad, so they wiped out all the airbenders. Aang, you are the Last Airbender."

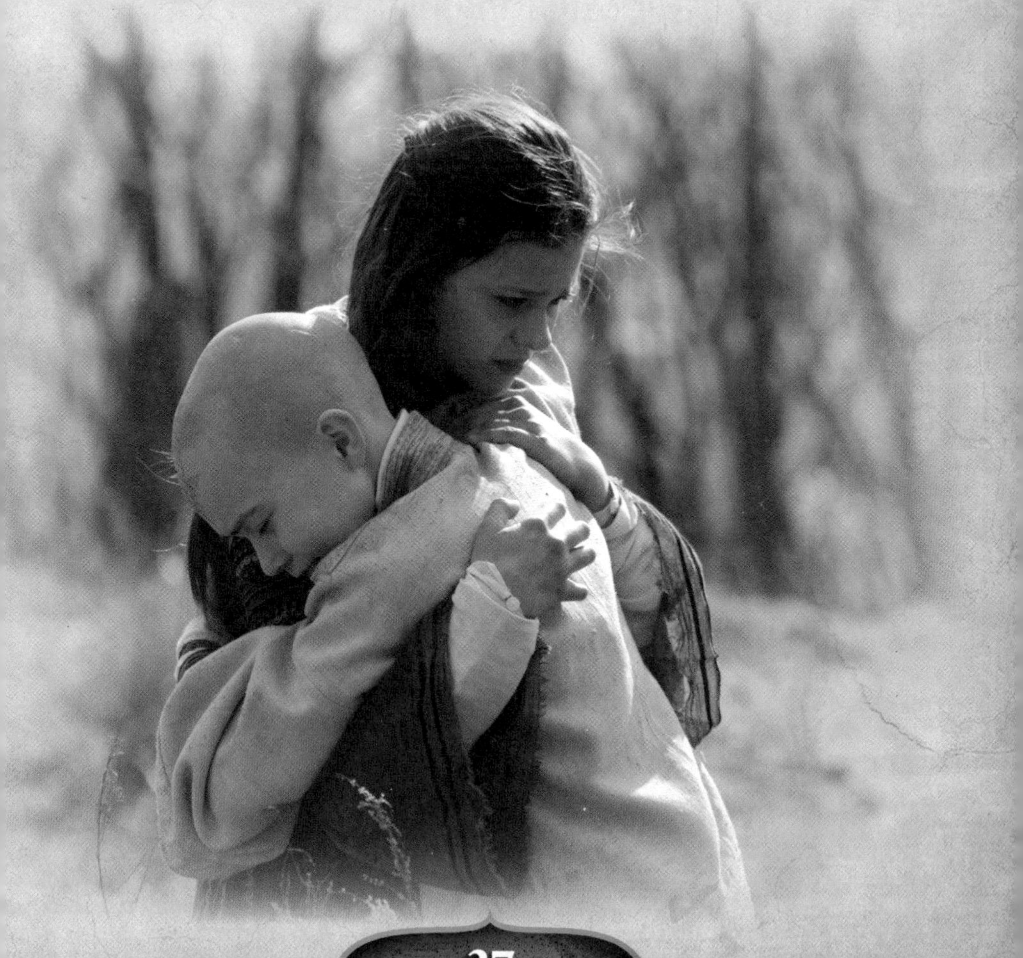

CHAPTER FIVE

Aang was quiet for a while. He could not believe what had happened.

"How much does the Fire Nation control?" he finally asked.

"A lot," Katara answered. "Most of the villages in the Earth Kingdom. They haven't been able to conquer any big cities yet, but I'm sure they are making plans."

"The monks told me that I was the Avatar," Aang said. "They said I would never have a family. So I ran away before they trained me to be the Avatar. I only know how to bend air. I don't know how to bend the other elements."

"What if we find people to teach you?" Sokka asked.

Aang agreed that was the best plan, so they headed north to learn waterbending from the masters in the Northern Water Tribe.

On the way there, Aang asked the Dragon Spirit for help. How could he beat the Fire Nation? The spirit replied: *You must show them the power of water. They have forgotten that all elements are equal. The Avatar exists to prove that this is true.*

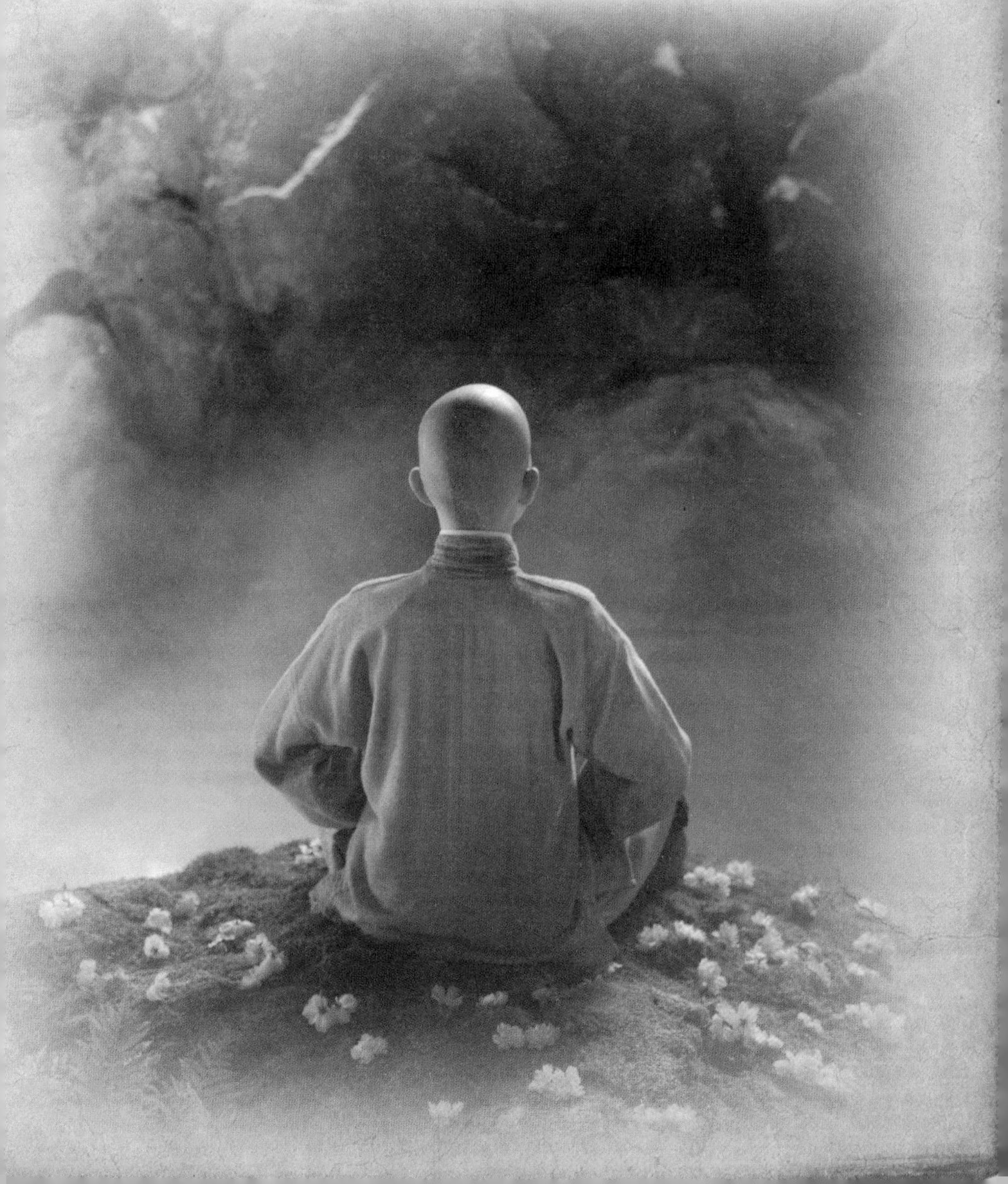

As they traveled through the Earth Kingdom, Katara, Sokka, and Aang were captured by Fire Nation soldiers.

They were thrown into a prison with some earthbenders.

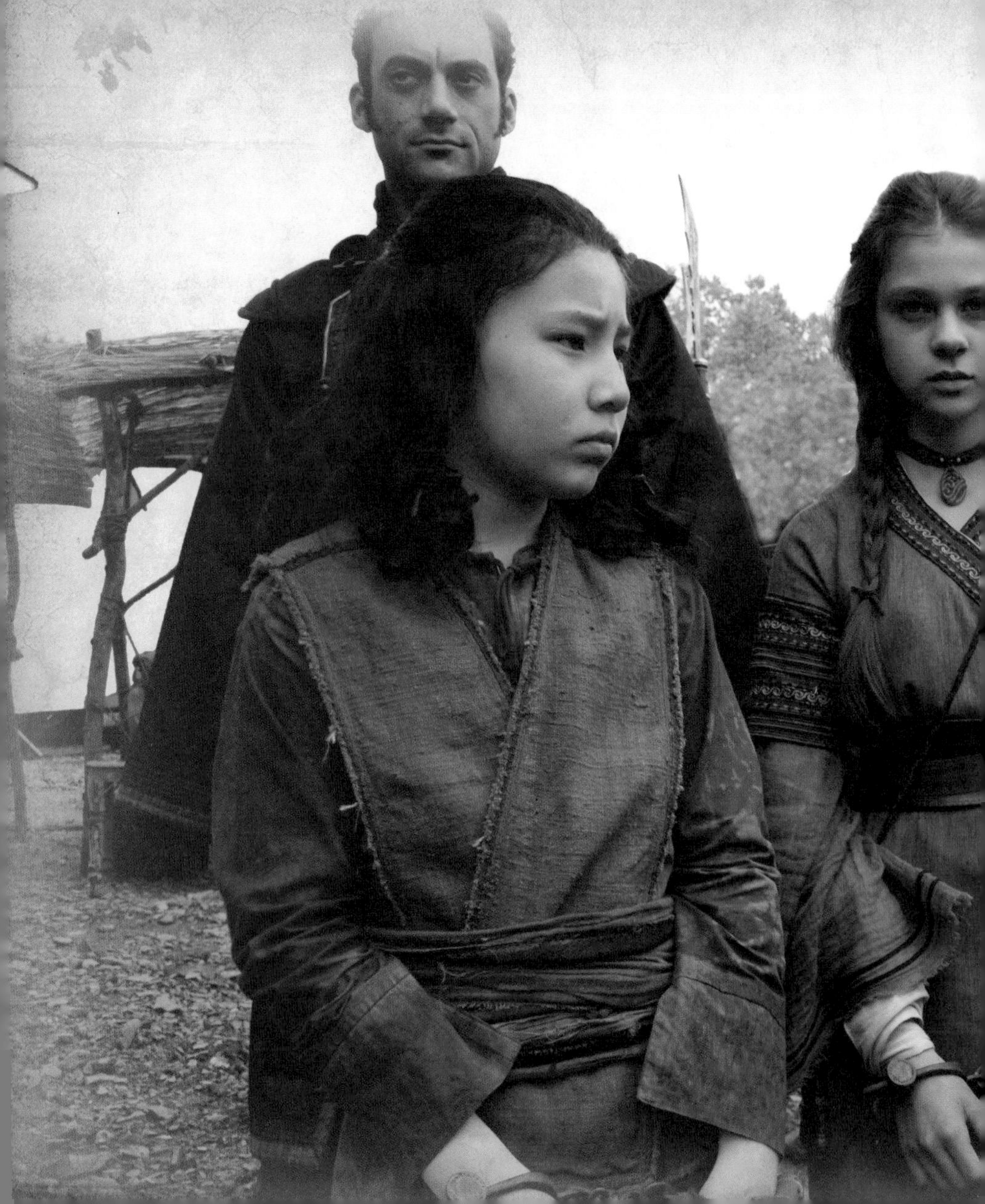

Aang could not believe that the earthbenders were not fighting back. He learned that it was because the firebenders were controlling them—and that without the Avatar, they had lost all hope.

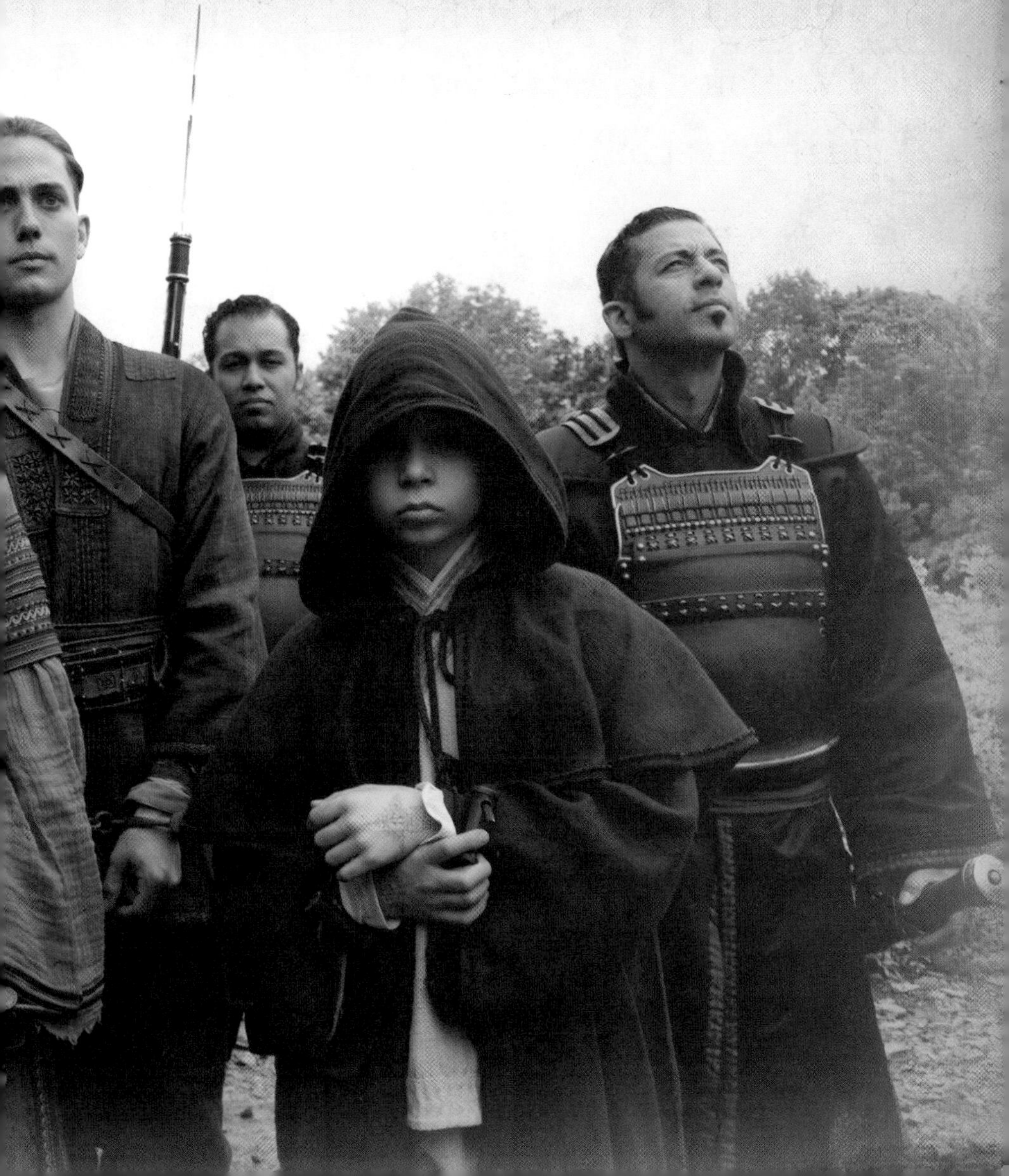

"The Avatar is dead," one prisoner said.

"If he was here, he would protect us!" said another.

Aang looked around. He now knew what he had to do. He didn't want the people to be defeated by the Fire Nation any longer. He could use his powers to help them.

"My name is Aang," he said proudly. "And I *am* the Avatar."

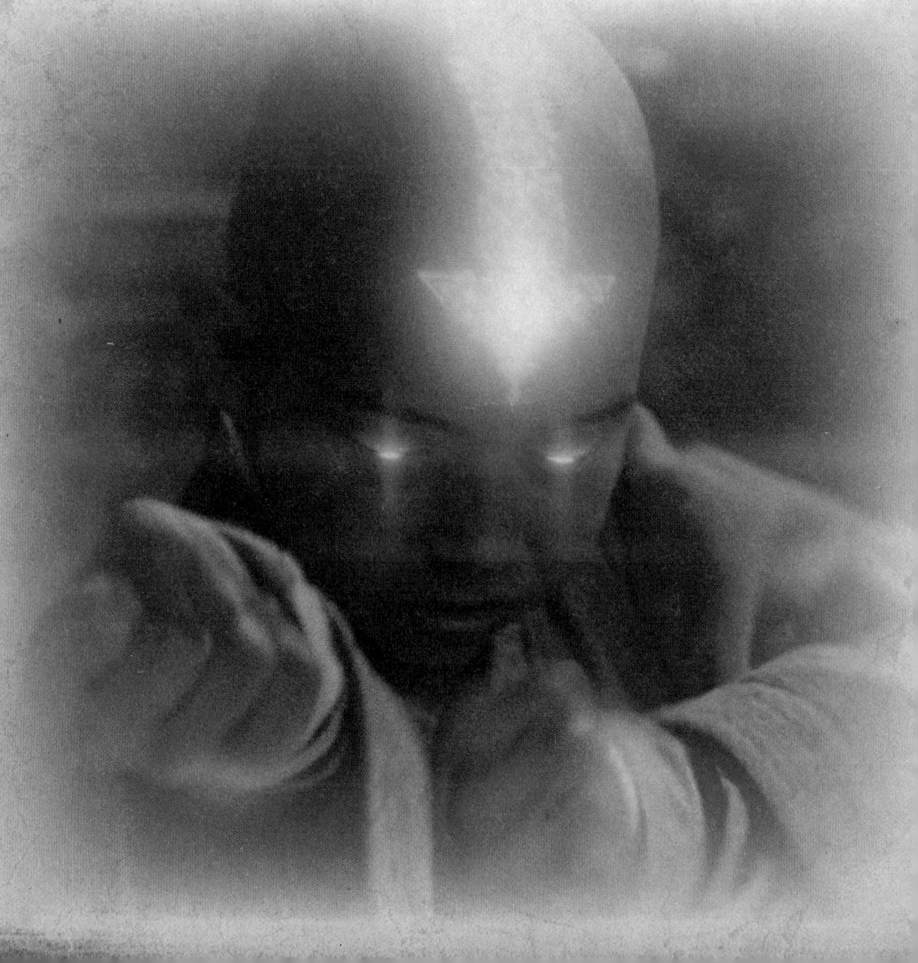